The Ruum and Other
Science Fiction Stories

Other book collections by Arthur Porges:

The Ruum and Other Science Fiction Stories

Arthur Porges

Edited by Richard Simms

Richard Simms Publications

This paperback first edition published in 2010

Richard Simms Publications, Surrey, England

ISBN: 978-0-9556942-6-4

With special thanks to Sue Wakefield, Cele Porges and Joel Hoffman.

For more information please visit The Arthur Porges Fan Site:

http://arthurporges.atwebpages.com

Contents

Introduction

If science fiction can be described as a literature of ideas, then Arthur Porges was well placed to make a significant contribution to the field. From an early age he read widely and voraciously, particularly of science, absorbing numerous books on natural history, physics and so on, while storing in his mind many little-known facts that he was later able to draw upon for his stories. This was indeed his specialty: for the possession of knowledge is one thing, but being able to manipulate an obscure scientific fact and work it into a plot for a short story was surely Porges' greatest gift as an author.

He was greatly influenced also by the science fiction he read while still at school. As a teenager growing up in Chicago, Porges, like most science fiction writers of his generation, was an avid reader of the American pulp magazines *Amazing Stories*, *Astounding* and *Weird Tales*. Having already devoured the imaginative writings of Jules Verne and H. G. Wells, he was equally inspired to write his own stories by the trailblazing, futuristic fiction of such pioneers of the genre as Edmond Hamilton, E. E. "Doc" Smith and Stanley G. Weinbaum.

As with his crime and mystery output, the kind of science fiction Porges himself ended up writing was for the most part based on original ideas and clever plot devices. As you will discover in the stories collected in this volume, he flourished in the realm of "hard" science fiction—a sub-genre that many consider represents the medium in its purest form. Porges' output in this field followed the dictates of the author Fredric Brown's neat definition of what science fiction actually represents (as opposed to fantasy): "Fantasy deals with things that are not and that cannot be. Science fiction deals with things that can be, that someday may be." The science fiction of Arthur Porges is largely concerned with what could quite reasonably happen in the future (or at least the future as envisaged by an author writing in the 1950s and '60s). A future probable given certain assumptions and extrapolations that have a basis in the scientific fact of today—in other words, possibilities with roots that are confined within the realms of logic.

It could be argued that his output in this genre was not necessarily akin to the work of better-known practitioners of "hard" science fiction. Several of his contemporaries were more expansive for one thing; Raymond F. Jones and Hal Clement wrote novels as well as short fiction, whereas Porges famously concentrated solely on the latter form. His contributions to the field might best be described as "microcosmic" by comparison, the majority of his stories concerned with small-scale, localized incidents set on our home planet. You will find no galaxy-spanning sagas, space armadas, planetary romances or epic off-world adventures among his stories. Moreover several of Porges' concise exercises in science fiction literature were perhaps a little too quirky, too much his own to be comparable with the works of his contemporaries. Nevertheless, a love of science was what fundamentally drove him to write science fiction. As previously noted, one cannot stress enough how most of his meticulously researched science fiction was heavily slanted towards obscure scientific trivia, ingeniously transmogrified by the author into the bare bones of his deftly contrived plots.

Another side to his writing in this medium was humor. Porges was not averse to writing the odd farcical science fiction comedy, or even some intentionally wacky tales that bordered on space opera. He was also apt to write the kind of fantastic yarn that falls somewhere between fantasy and science fiction; such hard to categorize entries in the Porges canon blur the distinction between the two genres. The reader will find examples of these kinds of stories within the pages of this volume, the background of which perhaps warrants some explanation at this point.

In recent years Mike Ashley and myself have ensured that Porges' fantasy and horror writings are well represented in book form. Almost his entire output in these genres can now be found in the collections *The Mirror and Other Strange Reflections* (Ash-Tree Press, 2002) and *The Devil and Simon Flagg and Other Fantastic Tales* (Richard Simms Publications, 2009).

Unfortunately his science fiction has been less well served. True, a fair number of the stories he wrote in this field have been anthologized down the years, but to date the only dedicated science fiction collection is the book *Eight Problems in Space: The Ensign De Ruyter Stories* (2008). This book, available direct from its Canadian publisher (The Battered Silicon Dispatch Box), assembles a series of inter-connected "scientific problem" stories originally published in *Amazing Stories* and *Fantastic* over forty years ago. However the balance of Arthur Porges' science fiction has remained uncollected until now.

Porges wrote the majority of his science fiction in the 1950s and 1960s, his most prolific period of writing. In assembling this body of work for republication in book form—with the happy addition of two unpublished gems that will see print for the first time—I have elected to divide these stories into two separate collections, one for each decade. We start with this volume, which covers the 1950s period. An additional rationale behind this book is to provide the reader with a selection of stories that illustrate his early development as a published writer while also offering a sound introduction to his work in this medium.

By the time he had started out as a professional writer in the early 1950s, Porges, now in his thirties, had largely honed his writing skills. He had cut his teeth two decades earlier by attending a writing course at The Lewis Institute in Chicago. Years later he was to learn a tough lesson about the ins and outs of manuscript formatting. In the late 1940s a succession of his stories were turned down by various markets, largely due to the fact that his manuscripts failed to conform to the requirements of magazine editors: double-spacing, word counts, etc.

As soon as Porges realized where he was going wrong he quickly rectified this shortcoming and the rejection slips stopped coming. In 1950, Porges finally started selling his work to magazines. At this time he was writing stories as a sideline while still holding down a job as a college teacher of mathematics in Los Angeles. Most of his early science fiction sales in the first half of the decade were to *The Magazine of Fantasy and Science Fiction* (from hereon referred to as *F&SF*). At the helm of this fledgling monthly publication were the editors Anthony Boucher and J. Francis McComas. Boucher in particular was a powerful influence on Porges. The multi-talented Boucher, an author, book critic and magazine editor rolled into one, found the time to provide those who submitted their work to *F&SF* with both encouragement and constructive criticism. Porges was no exception; as a fledgling writer the invaluable guidance he gained through correspondence with Boucher benefited his writing profoundly. Taking the editor's helpful suggestions on board, he managed to revise some of his first manuscripts into what were to become some of his best-known stories. In later years Porges was to cite the working relationship he had with Boucher as the most meaningful interaction he was ever to enjoy with an editor.

When it came to the rewriting and general development of "The Ruum" (1953), the opening story of this collection, the relationship between author and editor almost amounted to a partnership. As indeed it did with the famous Porges fantasy "The Devil and Simon Flagg" (1952), also published in *F&SF*, although through the years "The Ruum" has achieved an even greater fame.

The story of Boucher's input with regards to putting the finishing touches on this outstanding story is interesting in itself. "The Ruum" was not awarded a straightforward acceptance. After Porges had first submitted the story Boucher, having read it, decided that while he liked it well enough, he would write back to the author with the complaint that the story went too fast, that there was not enough sense of time passing. Porges agreed that his narrative would benefit from a little fleshing out and duly "padded" the text while managing to retain the sense of suspense that makes the story so readable to this day. Boucher in turn approved of the reworking and finally deemed it suitable for publication, including it in the October 1953 issue of his magazine.

You might say that the rest is history. "The Ruum" is quite simply Porges' best-known and most reprinted story. The plot itself is delightfully clever and yet simple at the same time. A lone prospector camped out in the Canadian Rockies comes across a motley collection of paralyzed animals, all preserved in a state of suspended animation. Most incredibly, these unfortunate creatures include a perfect specimen of a stegosaur! Shortly after this bewildering discovery a robot appears on the scene, intent on adding Jim Irwin to its bizarre collection. We are informed at the start of the story that this otherworldy spheroid is a Type H-9 Ruum, a specimen-gathering machine designed to capture and subdue local organisms, provided they fall within certain parameters. Its presence on Earth is explained by the fact that it was accidentally left behind in prehistoric times by the crew of a visiting alien spaceship, irreversibly on its way back to a distant star by the time the mistake is discovered.

Fast forward several million years and we find Jim Irwin, who is not equipped with such information, in a dire predicament. Although our protagonist is able to outrun his pursuer, the ruum will not give up. Nor will the robot be deterred from its purpose by the bullets from Irwin's high-powered rifle and the unsuccessful booby traps that he sets to disable it. What ensues is a chase story with an inventive twist, a suspenseful tale that commands the reader's attention right up to the pulse-quickening finale. Obviously one cannot give too much away here, but in later years Porges was amused to note how several people, perhaps not used to science fiction, didn't understand the ending: the all important final sentence.

"The Ruum" has obviously touched a lot of people that have read it in the decades since its original publication. One reason for its success might be that "The Ruum" is a quite beautiful example of pure science fiction. As Edmund Crispin so eloquently reflected, the story could never have worked if the robot had been anything other than what it was. In other words, take away the science fiction element and you cut out the heart, the whole point of Porges' tale.

The story's remarkable popularity might also be attributed to its inclusion in the English curriculum of the U.S. High School system. In fact many readers fondly recall their first encounter with "The Ruum" as required reading in the classroom—a situation still true today!

Furthermore, as noted earlier, it has seen several reprints, thus reaching a wider audience than any other of his stories. Since setting up the Porges website in 1999, I have received more emails about this story than any other, some from would-be filmmakers interested in acquiring adaptation rights although, at the time of writing, a movie version has yet to materialize. Porges was a little puzzled at the level of interest from this quarter, commenting in one of his letters to me that a modern-day treatment of his tale would have to be 90% special effects, and with only one human. He then went on to joke that Hollywood would no doubt team up his lone male protagonist with a female companion, both being chased by a relentless super-terminator machine. In all honesty I must say such a prospect makes me cringe. Let's hope a desecration of this kind never happens.

Finally, a somewhat unlikely influence "The Ruum" had on popular culture was recently brought to my attention. As a Pink Floyd fan I should really have spotted this … ever wondered what inspired the title of the Floyd's early psychedelic instrumental "Interstellar Overdrive"? Look no further than the first line of Arthur's story!

Before I continue to discuss the contents of this collection I should point out that the story of "The Ruum" doesn't quite end there. A superb sequel, explaining what happened to that unwavering robot after the events described in the first story, surfaced in the May 1960 issue of *F&SF*. For some unexplained reason, "A Specimen for the Queen" never took off and has remained unjustly out of print for fifty years. This lost classic is one of the pieces I will be including in the next book of Porges' science fiction stories.

In common with "The Ruum," the following six stories in this book are drawn from early 1950s issues of *F&SF*. In the past "The Rats" (1951) has been wrongly listed as Porges' first published story. That particular honor goes to the fantasy vignette "Modeled in Clay," sold to *Man to Man* magazine in 1950. Although "The Rats" was published in *F&SF*, this was in fact as a reprint; it initially appeared ten months earlier in the February 1951 issue of the magazine *Man's World*. Such are the details of the story's provenance.

It is hard to find any fault with "The Rats." It is up there with the author's very best: it boasts action, ingenuity, dramatic tension and the kind of realism and attention to detail that was to become Porges' trademark as a short story wizard. Given the emerging Cold War period in which this tale and others assembled here were written it is unsurprising that a number of these stories are informed by a fear of nuclear annihilation. In "The Rats" we are transported to a possible near future (or the then near future), where a doggedly self-reliant loner holes up in a remote, abandoned village in preparation for what seems inevitable—an all-out atomic war between the two superpowers. Armed and supplied with weapons and tinned foods, Jeffrey Clark finds the locality he has chosen as his last stand to be overrun with mutated rats.

A battle for survival between the solitary human and the horde of rats (whose intelligence has been enhanced by radioactivity from a nearby proving ground for nuclear weapons) is vividly depicted in this chilling tale. As the narrative progresses, Clark becomes increasingly unnerved by the unusually clever behavior his rodent enemies are beginning to exhibit. Porges' description of the rats and their unsettling activities, along with Clark's increasing unease, makes for chilling reading. There is one especially powerful scene where he discovers the rats have cunningly tried to utilize one of his own trap devices to kill *him*. The balance of power begins to turn …

As with "The Ruum" the following story opens with another lone hunter in the wilderness, armed with a Geiger counter and seeking deposits of valuable ores. But here any similarity between the two stories ends. "The Fly" (1952) is a concise account of what happens when a prospector encounters a rather unusual bluebottle that has been caught in a spider's web. In addition to being a highly original piece, "The Fly" is well written; even poetic at times, as this passage illustrates:

> Spiders are an ancient race; ages before man wrought wonders through his subtle abstractions of points and lines, a spiral not to be distinguished from this one winnowed the breezes of some prehistoric summer.

As for whether the science of the story holds up, Porges once recalled that "The Fly" had the distinction of being attacked, good-naturedly, by that true titan of science fiction, Isaac Asimov. In one of his essays Asimov asserted that the atom-powered device described in Porges' story was scientifically impossible because of its minute size. Porges accepted at the time that his esteemed critic had all the evidence in his favor. But in reconsidering his idea fifty years later, in the light of technological advances it became apparent that what he imagined in 1952 could one day conceivably come true. He highlighted the fact that as lasers are now able to manipulate atoms it was not unreasonable to assume that a superior civilization could drive hydrogen atoms in small numbers together to make a few helium atoms and a lot of energy. However Porges hastily qualified this statement with the modest declaration: "But I'm not the scientist by miles that Asimov was, so I could still be wrong!"

Interestingly, Porges went on to reflect: "Asimov and I had much in common: born about the same time, science degrees—he had a PhD, I a Masters, his in a top university, mine in a small, not-very-good one—both of us taught college courses, wrote science fiction, etc. But he was far more prolific, and wrote in several major fields."

We now come to a story very close to my heart. "By a Fluke" (1955) wasn't the first Porges story I read, but it was this one that got me truly hooked on his writings. I fell in love with the author's style, his rich descriptions, esoteric subject matter … I mean, what other writer do you know of that can take his knowledge of a liver fluke's strange life-cycle and coalesce it into fiction form? That is precisely what Porges achieves here in one of his most unusual and inventive science fiction stories.

Exquisitely crafted, "By a Fluke" is narrated by a type of parasitic flatworm. Yes, you read that right. At its heart the story is a cry of despair by an individual belonging to a race of organisms whose life span is all too brief. The narrator laments the cruel twist of fate that should house a brilliant mathematical mind in a short-lived, vulnerable and largely immobile body. For in Porges' story the liver fluke subspecies are sentient, telepathically able to communicate with each other and, on reaching maturity are gifted with the ability to philosophize and solve difficult mathematical problems. (As an aside, eagle-eyed Porges buffs will notice the reference to Fermat's Last Theorem, the famous mathematical enigma that crops up in several of his stories, most notably in "The Devil and Simon Flagg" (1952), wherein it is central to the plot.) Aware of mankind but unable to communicate with them, the liver flukes are frustrated in their attempts to make humans aware of their sentience. One individual of the race (the narrator of the story), close to death, recites its autobiography, hoping against hope that someone, anyone, out there might, by some miracle, receive its mental transmission.

"By a Fluke" is powerful stuff, right up to the final, devastating paragraph. It's easily one of his most imaginative stories. It also happens to be one of the best in the entire Porges canon and, if you will allow me a little rant, what a travesty this story has never been reprinted until now. I'm baffled as to why the science fiction anthologists of the time failed to pick up on this gem.

Putting such considerations to one side, the question of what inspired the author to write this piece will doubtless remain unanswered. But one can at least pinpoint the source of Porges' knowledge. Along with stories like "The Odyssey of Epeira" (1952) and "The Soulless Ones" (a very early piece published for the first time in 2008), for the accurate detail of "By a Fluke" Porges drew on his reading of the great French entomologist Jean-Henri Fabre's *Souvenirs Entomologiques*.

We stay in the realm of miniature-sized life-forms for what really *was* the very first Porges story I ever read, "Emergency Operation" (1956). In this case the central character is a microscopic alien surgeon called M'lo, who is injected into the bloodstream of a human patient to remove a radioactive fragment from within the patient's brain. Conventional methods of surgery are insufficient to perform this delicate and intricate medical task. Microsurgery, in situ, is the only answer, so a collaborative effort with a member of a friendly alien race is necessary. M'lo, who happens to be smaller than a pinhead, is a highly skilled surgeon from a planet circling Procyon. "Emergency Operation" is the story of his adventure inside a human body as he races against time to locate the deadly isotope and save the patient's life. This fascinating tale has a documentary-style realism about it, an opulence of accurate detail that endows it with power and authenticity.

The "microscopic world" setting was of course nothing new when Porges wrote "Emergency Operation," but his treatment of the theme was unique. One item of trivia that cropped up in my correspondence with him was the similarity of his idea to that which surfaced ten years later as the basis of the feature film *Fantastic Voyage* (1966). Porges wondered if the filmmakers may have drawn inspiration from his plot, but recognized that it would be hard to prove anything and, for all he knew, another science fiction writer may have come up with the same idea before him.

While "Emergency Operation" was reprinted on one occasion, I see this minor classic is another story that has been out of print for many years so I am delighted to present it here to a new audience. The same goes for the hilarious "Story Conference" (1953), which also features a being from another world. Unlike the previous story, this one's a riotous spoof with an audacious premise. A Martian poet crash lands on Earth and finds he is stranded. Blending in with human society, he unsuccessfully attempts to make a living from writing poetry. Hell, that's hard to do whatever your planet of origin! Our immigrant from Mars then decides to apply his creative talents to the writing of science fiction stories. After all, being able to write about life on the red planet with the unique asset of first-hand experience should place him head and shoulders above the rest of the field, right? Surely, our Martian castaway reasons, such knowledge will imbue his ostensibly imaginative writing with an authority the editor of *Sober Science Fiction* (read *Astounding*) magazine will find impossible to ignore.

How misguided poor Gryzzll Pfrafnik (a.k.a Mr. Smith) is proven to be! The setting for this story is a heated meeting between the Martian and the editor of *Sober Science Fiction*, who proceeds to explain why he can't buy Pfrafnik's story, on the grounds of the poorly handled science. Much to his frustration, the budding author's protestations fall on deaf ears. The biological and social details that Pfrafnik puts in his story, relating specifically to his own race, the dominant life-form on Mars, are considered by the editor as far too unrealistic for the discerning readers of *Sober Science Fiction*.

"Story Conference" is patently a meditation on the exacting demands readers of "hard" science fiction in the early 1950s put upon authors, connoisseurs who thought they knew it all and, along with editors, refused to accept anything about Mars that didn't conform to the conventional theories of the period. A writer needed to research his material carefully, to get his speculations within the realms of what was considered "right," lest the fury of the scientifically literate magazine's readership descend on the hapless author's head. In a nutshell, any lapse in scientific accuracy was liable to land a careless writer in trouble with readers. Much to his increasing chagrin, our Martian wordsmith soon discovers that the kind of story he is trying to pitch would never get past any self-respecting science fiction editor.

"Story Conference" reminds me a good deal of the opening portion of Fredric Brown's affectionate spoof science fiction novel *What Mad Universe* (1949), with its fun and knowing tongue-in-cheek references to typical genre magazine titles of the time. In Porges' story we have *Thrilling Space* and *Shocking Wonder*, whereas Brown comes up with *Surprising Stories* in his outstanding novel. Apart from this aspect and despite its undoubtedly being something of a period piece, what makes "Story Conference" so enjoyable still is that it exhibits one of Porges' main strengths as a writer: his ear for good dialogue. What he lacked in rounded characters, psychological complexities and the subtle nuances of human relations he more than made up for in the kind of barbed verbal exchanges on display in "Story Conference," an intriguing yarn that should raise a wry smile.

The rather anachronistic "The Logic of Rufus Weir" (1955) is the last story in this collection derived from the pages of *F&SF*. A bit of an oddity this one. The plot is set in a near future that the author envisaged back in 1955 which frankly—without putting too fine a point on it—never made it to the present. (Perhaps it is too easy for us, half a century later, to laugh in hindsight at what a science fiction author got wrong.) The tale is a chronicle of a series of interplanetary experiments conducted by the scientific genius Rufus Weir. His mission is to colonize Venus with a vanguard of various animals to see how long they can survive on Earth's sister planet. After several test runs, rocket ships carrying mice, hamsters, guinea pigs, rabbits and monkeys are successfully landed on Venus. In time this group of lesser animals establish a colony on the cloud-wrapped planet, a combination of lesser gravity and radiation endowing them greater size, intelligence and the power of speech. Weir decides to pay them a visit.

Admittedly the datedness of "The Logic of Rufus Weir" reveals itself all too easily to even the casual reader who does not care two hoots about astronomy. There is a reference, for example, to the "pilotless moon rocket of 1986," as well as the inescapable fact that this was written at a time when nothing at all was known of the surface conditions on Venus. We are now aware of course that no life, at least as we know it, can possibly exist in such a harsh environment.

Having said that, there is still much to admire here, not least the black humor. Porges obviously did not intend Rufus Weir as an endearing character, but one cannot help but admire his unfazed reaction to what he finds when he lands on Venus. As the title suggests, the story revolves around his unassailable logic; an unfaltering devotion to the higher cause of scientific progress, no matter what the cost. Incidentally, Weir's steadfast intellectual detachment and "logical inferences" bring to mind Porges' wheelchair-bound detective Cyriack Skinner Grey, who appeared in a series of mystery stories now collected in the book *The Curious Cases of Cyriack Skinner Grey* (2009).

"The Entity" (1955) and "Whirlpool" (1957) were the only stories Porges sold to *Fantastic Universe* magazine. Both are reprinted here for the first time and are truly excellent in different ways.

"The Entity" is startling and inventive. It might even be the most accomplished of all the stories assembled here. A tale of humanity's first contact with an alien race, the narrative develops along unexpected lines as the visiting extraterrestrial emissary explains his mission to a gathering of the world's leaders. The story he relates is a strange one. Out in the far reaches of space, the envoy's own civilization had, in the distant past, ensnared with force fields an unknown entity that was passing through their solar system. This creature proved totally alien to them, unresponsive to attempts at contact, and in possession of an unfathomable physical structure. Moreover, despite long study its method of absorbing or using energy remained incomprehensible. Concluding that this inscrutable being must have traveled from a galaxy at the far edge of the universe, the emissary's race continued to observe it over a period of millions of years, until an error freed the entity to once again roam across intergalactic space. After the passing of countless millennia, the creature's former captors finally succeed in tracking it down. They discover that this vast, intangible entity has settled on the Earth, where it has resided since the planet was a molten mass. At the culmination of his speech, the emissary from another galaxy has a question to ask of the world's representatives. An enigma that is inextricably tied in with the exact nature of this alien elemental and how it relates to life on Earth.

"The Entity" is a wildly imaginative, cleverly structured science fiction story that makes for enthralling reading. It builds with a relentless logic towards its provocative conclusion, an ending that asks a difficult, possibly unanswerable question of the reader. I simply stand in awe of this story; to my mind no amount of praise can do this underrated classic justice.

In "Whirlpool" Porges, in typical fashion, takes a little-known fact from the world of physics and works it brilliantly into a plot device from which he can build a story. A tense little thriller, "Whirlpool" is set in the future. Joel Craima is the hero of the story, held captive by religious fanatics in a nuclear power plant. There are only two of these reactors on the face of the globe, one for each hemisphere. His captors intend to bring about Judgement Day by blowing up the atomic pile and setting off a chain reaction in the atmosphere that could destroy the planet. The fate of mankind itself hangs in the balance as Craima quickly realizes that, although he's in a position to secretly alert the authorities and thereby prevent the calamity from occurring, it is imperative he answers a key question—which of the two reactors is he in, North or South? Porges hits on an ingenious solution to the hero's dilemma, and also uses his tale to take a characteristic stab at religious fanaticism; as a fellow skeptic I find it easy to empathize with the author's sentiment.

In one of his letters to me Porges made it clear he wasn't overly keen on this story. While acknowledging the cleverness of his gimmick, he dismissed the story itself as a "potboiler." For some time my memory of reading "Whirlpool" concurred with this. But I was wrong. On rereading it for the purposes of this book, I found it was well written, with pace, excitement, and altogether a thoroughly satisfying read.

"The Unwilling Professor" made its sole appearance in the January 1954 issue of *Dynamic Science Fiction* magazine. I have to wonder if Porges would have been willing to see it given another airing, as it is another of those stories he didn't rate too highly—although he once confessed to taking a guilty pleasure in it! Putting that to one side, the story's inclusion in this particular magazine is of some contextual interest.

Every writer is a hostage to their time, and Porges was one of a generation of short story specialists (writers like Henry Slesar and Edward D. Hoch) who came on the scene in the dying days of the pulp magazines. *Dynamic Science Fiction* was one of the few science fiction pulp magazines remaining. At the end of the 1950s they had died out completely or, as was the case with *Astounding* and *Amazing Stories*, had long since converted to digest-size format. The pulps were killed by other, more fashionable diversions—television and the burgeoning market for cheap paperbacks. It is my belief that if Porges had begun his published writing career a few years earlier, his stories would have been printed in many more pulp issues. By the time he had sold "The Unwilling Professor," the once-great pulps were entering their death throes.

The story itself is an enchanting romp, a deliciously screwball science fiction comedy about an alien ambassador from Venus whose spaceship lands in the grounds of a college campus on Earth. Professor Slakmak, who happens to resemble a rabbit, introduces himself to the first humans he happens to meet. It is his bad luck that chance brings him into contact with two obnoxious teenage students, perennial underachievers who proceed to kidnap him and exploit the Venusian's superior knowledge of math to better their grades. I admit the scenes where the young morons abuse their reluctant alien tutor did have me grinding my teeth, just a little. But I needn't have worried, for Porges' sympathies lay not with these sorry excuses for human beings but with their captive, the likeable visitor from another world who you desperately want to win the day. "The Unwilling Professor" is a satisfying slice of humor that is very much of its time.

As with the previous story, "Guilty as Charged" (1955) found an unusual outlet. It was first published in *The New York Post*, one of the very few pieces Porges sold to a newspaper. In this memorable story two scientists use an ingenious contraption to look, as through a television screen, two hundred years into the future. They focus on a courtroom scene, witnessing across the gulf of time what is obviously the trial of a woman accused of a crime they can only guess at, as it is impossible for them to augment the image they scrutinize with any sound from the judicial proceedings. Such is the premise of this remarkable piece, which boasts a shocking twist at the end of the story. "Guilty as Charged" was good enough to merit several reprints, including one in the hardbound compilation *The Best Science Fiction Stories and Novels: 1955*, edited by T. E. Dikty. Incidentally Dikty, working in partnership with Everett F. Bleiler, had the discernment to anthologize two other Porges stories, "The Fly" and "The Rats," both featured earlier on in this volume.

The only previously unpublished story I have included here was penned at some point in the late 1950s (the manuscript is undated) at a time when Porges had recently retired from teaching to become a full-time freelance writer. "The Mannering Report" also concerns time. In this case a pioneering physicist travels back over 100,000 years into the Earth's past. The story of Sir Walter Mannering's experience is carefully constructed, each fact logically presented to the reader in the form of an extraordinary report read out to the enthralled attendees of a scientific conference.

Ornamented with typical Porgesian touches, the idea at the core of "The Mannering Report" is one I have not come across anywhere else in my reading of science fiction. In this measured and convincingly detailed story, Porges raises the possibility that mankind's technological advancements cannot exist before their proper time. The electrical circuits and machinery that the time-travelling scientist attempts to build in the far past fail to work, despite his mechanical competence and the dictates of logic. The theory Porges proposes in this provocative tale is that in prehistoric times, countless years before the Industrial Revolution and its associated inventions, the intangible and immutable fabric of the universe simply will not allow such displacement. Porges speculates with some authority that perhaps, just perhaps, things must occur in their natural order.

Considering the quality of "The Mannering Report," it is impossible to know for sure why this story went unsold. I never had the chance to ask Arthur about it and he may not have received any feedback from editors anyway, his work being submitted through an agent at the time this was written. It may well have been rejected on the grounds of a lack of dramatic tension, but I could be way off the mark in assuming that. For myself, I considered it worthy of publication the minute I read it!

The final two stories are from 1959. "Security" and "A Touch of Sun" originally appeared in the Ziff-Davis owned magazines *Amazing Stories* and *Fantastic* respectively. Cele Goldsmith was the editor of these titles when Porges began to submit his work to this particular market. Both stories represent the beginning of what was to be a very prolific period in Porges' career, one that would last until the mid-1960s, a successful era I have long labeled his "Golden Age" of writing. Goldsmith bought a string of Porges stories during her editorial reign, regularly placing his quirky fantasy and science fiction yarns in the pages of both magazines, alongside those of other talented purveyors of unusual short fiction. These included exceptional writers such as Robert F. Young and David R. Bunch.

Porges' writing blossomed in this reliable outlet. "Security" represents the very best of the science fiction tales he contributed to Goldsmith. Another story that has the Cold War and the threat of a nuclear conflict as its backdrop, this near future thriller is a chilly, paranoid examination of the nature of military security, with regards to the need to keep certain scientific information out of the hands of an enemy power.

The action takes place in a laboratory within a military base, presumably located somewhere in the United States. A top research scientist and a commander discuss various aspects of security, mindful of the valuable scientific information housed inside Dr. Mason's brain. Information the enemy superpower (referred to in this story as the "Sino-Soviets") would dearly love to acquire. Mason holds the key to the balance of power, and is guarded by military intelligence to within an inch of his life. Surrounded by layers of high-tech security, with all the angles seemingly covered, Mason is a virtual prisoner, forbidden any outside contact, his loneliness assuaged only by a pet cat. No enemy agent could possibly get to him, the commander is supremely confident of that. But the spy is closer than they could ever guess …

"Security" is a master class in structure and brevity, a story that cemented Porges' growing reputation as a highly respected practitioner of short science fiction. It is an honor to republish it here. I hope you enjoy it as much as I did.

To round off this collection it gives me great pleasure to present the result of a one-off collaboration between Arthur and his older brother Irwin Porges. The pivotal character in "A Touch of Sun" is an eccentric ex-professor who has lived as a hermit in a wooden shack on the edge of a desert ranch for forty years. His world is turned upside down when an electronics company decides to build a television-relay tower on the site of his home. Seeing his beloved abode destroyed in the name of progress and watching the structure as it is slowly erected in its place is bad enough. Add to that the bullying taunts of the chief engineer of the construction gang assigned to the job, and the crotchety old recluse is moved to anger. There are some nice human touches to this story, such as the victim's inability to defend himself with any verbal coherence; the result of a life of solitude. As Porges deadpans: "The nerve paths joining brain and vocal chords had almost atrophied through disuse."

As the narrative unfolds, Professor Tincan—so nicknamed by his unsympathetic tormentor for his unusual hobby of collecting aluminum tin cans—vows revenge, if only to restore some self-esteem. And his promise is not an idle one, for he has something up his sleeve, an ingenious trick that utilizes his knowledge of applied math and physics. In typical Porges fashion, the true highlight of "A Touch of Sun" is the inventive manipulation of the physical environment, the deft employment of what materials there are to hand. Tin cans, for instance.

This poignant story showcases some great humor and dialogue. With regards to the nature of his brother's contribution, Porges once remarked that Irwin "knew nothing of science." But though the minutiae of Irwin Porges' involvement will most probably remain a mystery forever, having read several of his excellent mystery short stories, I suspect much of the dialogue, characterization and story structure could well have been his doing.

And so, until *The Rescuer and Other Science Fiction Stories*, which will assemble his 1960s output in this genre, have fun reading the stories in this book. Revel in the cleverness of the ideas, the imagination, tight-writing style, briskly delineated characters and sharp dialogue. Qualities that elevate these stories above the ordinary. Science fiction by a master storyteller, as fresh and vital today as when these tales were written over half a century ago.

A touch of sun? No. A touch of genius.

Richard Simms
Surrey, England
July, 2010

The Ruum

The cruiser *Ilkor* had just gone into her interstellar overdrive beyond the orbit of Pluto when a worried officer reported to the Commander.

"Excellency," he said uneasily, "I regret to inform you that because of a technician's carelessness, a Type H-9 Ruum has been left behind on the third planet, together with anything it may have collected."

The Commander's triangular eyes hooded momentarily, but when he spoke his voice was level.

"How was the ruum set?"

"For a maximum radius of 30 miles, and 160 pounds plus or minus fifteen."

There was silence for several seconds, then the Commander said: "We cannot reverse course now. In a few weeks we'll be returning, and can pick up the ruum then. I do not care to have one of those costly, self-energizing models charged against my ship. You will see," he ordered coldly, "that the individual responsible is severely punished."

But at the end of its run, in the neighborhood of Rigel, the cruiser met a flat, ring-shaped raider; and when the inevitable fire-fight was over, both ships, semi-molten, radioactive, and laden with dead, were starting a billion year orbit around the star.

And on the Earth, it was the age of reptiles.

When the two men had unloaded the last of the supplies, Jim Irwin watched his partner climb into the little seaplane. He waved at Walt.

"Don't forget to mail that letter to my wife," Jim shouted.

"The minute I land," Walt Leonard called back, starting to rev the engine. "And you find us some uranium—a strike is just what Cele needs. A fortune for your son and her, hey?" His white teeth flashed in a grin. "Don't rub noses with any grizzlies—shoot 'em, but don't scare 'em to death!"

Jim thumbed his nose as the seaplane speeded up, leaving a frothy wake. He felt a queer chill as the amphibian took off. For three weeks he would be isolated in this remote valley of the Canadian Rockies. If for any reason the plane failed to return to the icy blue lake, he would surely die. Even with enough food, no man could surmount the frozen peaks and make his way on foot over hundreds of miles of almost virgin wilderness. But of course Walt Leonard would return on schedule, and it was up to Jim whether or not they lost their stake. If there was any uranium in the valley, he had twenty-one days to find it. To work then, and no gloomy forebodings.

Moving with the unhurried precision of an experienced woodsman, he built a lean-to in the shelter of a rocky overhang. For this three weeks of summer, nothing more permanent was needed. Perspiring in the strong morning sun, he piled his supplies back under the ledge, well covered by a waterproof tarpaulin, and protected from the larger animal prowlers. All but the dynamite; that he cached, also carefully wrapped against moisture, 200 yards away. Only a fool shares his quarters with a box of high explosives.

The first two weeks went by all too swiftly, without any encouraging finds. There was only one good possibility left, and just enough time to explore it. So early one morning towards the end of his third week, Jim Irwin prepared for a last-ditch foray into the northeast part of the valley, a region he had not yet visited.

He took the Geiger counter, slipping on the earphones reversed, to keep the normal rattle from dulling his hearing, and reaching for the rifle, set out, telling himself it was now or never so far as this particular expedition was concerned. The bulky .30-06 was a nuisance and he had no enthusiasm for its weight, but the huge grizzlies of Canada are not intruded upon with impunity, and take a lot of killing. He'd already had to dispose of two, a hateful chore, since the big bears were vanishing all too fast. And the rifle had proved a great comfort on several ticklish occasions when actual firing had been avoided. The .22 pistol he left in its sheepskin holster in the lean-to.

He was whistling at the start, for the clear, frosty air, the bright sun on blue-white ice fields, and the heady smell of summer, all delighted his heart despite his bad luck as a prospector. He planned to go one day's journey to the new region, spend about 36 hours exploring it intensively, and be back in time to meet the plane at noon. Except for his emergency packet, he took no food or water. It would be easy enough to knock over a rabbit, and the streams were alive with firm-fleshed rainbow trout of the kind no longer common in the States.

All morning Jim walked, feeling an occasional surge of hope as the counter chattered. But its clatter always died down. The valley had nothing radioactive of value, only traces. Apparently they'd made a bad choice. His cheerfulness faded. They needed a strike badly, especially Walt. And his own wife, Cele, with a kid on the way. But there was still a chance. These last 36 hours—he'd snoop at night, if necessary—might be the pay-off. He reflected a little bitterly that it would help quite a bit if some of those birds he'd staked would make a strike and return his dough. Right this minute there was close to 8,000 bucks owing to him.

A wry smile touched his lips, and he abandoned unprofitable speculations for plans about lunch. The sun, as well as his stomach, said it was time. He had just decided to take out his line and fish a foaming brook, when he rounded a grassy knoll to come upon a sight that made him stiffen to a halt, his jaw dropping.

It was like some enterprising giant's outdoor butcher shop: a great assortment of animal bodies, neatly lined up in a triple row that extended almost as far as the eye could see. And what animals! To be sure, those nearest him were ordinary deer, bear, cougars, and mountain sheep—one of each, apparently—but down the line were strange, uncouth, half-formed, hairy beasts; and beyond them a nightmare conglomeration of reptiles. One of the latter, at the extreme end of the remarkable display, he recognized at once. There had been a much larger specimen fabricated about an incomplete skeleton, of course, in the museum at home.

No doubt about it—it was a small stegosaur, no bigger than a pony!

Fascinated, Jim walked down the line, glancing back over the immense array. Peering more closely at one scaly, dirty-yellow lizard, he saw an eyelid tremble. Then he realized the truth. The animals were not dead, but paralyzed and miraculously preserved. Perspiration prickled his forehead. How long since stegosaurs had roamed this valley?

All at once he noticed another curious circumstance: the victims were roughly of a size. Nowhere, for example, was there a really large saurian. No tyrannosaurus. For that matter, no mammoth. Each specimen was about the size of a large sheep. He was pondering this odd fact, when the underbrush rustled a warning behind him.

Jim Irwin had once worked with mercury, and for a second it seemed to him that a half-filled leather sack of the liquid metal had rolled into the clearing. For the quasi-spherical object moved with just such a weighty, fluid motion. But it was not leather; and what appeared at first a disgusting wartiness, turned out on closer scrutiny to be more like the functional projections of some outlandish mechanism. Whatever the thing was, he had little time to study it, for after the spheroid had whipped out and retracted a number of metal rods with bulbous, lens-like structures at their tips, it rolled towards him at a speed of about five miles an hour. And from its purposeful advance, the man had no doubt that it meant to add him to the pathetic heap of living-dead specimens.

Uttering an incoherent exclamation, Jim sprang back a number of paces, unslinging his rifle. The ruum that had been left behind was still some 30 yards off, approaching at that moderate but invariable velocity, an advance more terrifying in its regularity than the headlong charge of a mere brute beast.

Jim's hand flew to the bolt, and with practiced deftness he slammed a cartridge into the chamber. He snuggled the battered stock against his cheek, and using the peep sight, aimed squarely at the leathery bulk—a perfect target in the bright afternoon sun. A grim little smile touched his lips as he squeezed the trigger. He knew what one of those 180-grain, metal-jacketed, boat-tail slugs could do at

2,700 feet per second. Probably at this close range it would keyhole and blow the foul thing into a mush, by God!

Wham! The familiar kick against his shoulder. E-e-e-e-! The whining screech of a ricochet. He sucked in his breath. There could be no doubt whatever. At a mere twenty yards, a bullet from this hard-hitting rifle had glanced from the ruum's surface.

Frantically Jim worked the bolt. He blasted two more rounds, then realized the utter futility of such tactics. When the ruum was six feet away, he saw gleaming finger-hooks flick from warty knobs, and a hollow, sting-like probe, dripping greenish liquid, poised snakily between them. The man turned and fled.

Jim Irwin weighed exactly 149 pounds.

It was easy enough to pull ahead. The ruum seemed incapable of increasing its speed. But Jim had no illusions on that score. The steady five-mile-an-hour pace was something no organism on Earth could maintain for more than a few hours. Before long, Jim guessed, the hunted animal had either turned on its implacable pursuer or, in the case of more timid creatures, ran itself to exhaustion in a circle out of sheer panic. Only the winged were safe. But for anything on the ground the result was inevitable: another specimen for the awesome array. And for whom the whole collection? Why? Why?

Coolly, as he ran, Jim began to shed all surplus weight. He glanced at the reddening sun, wondering about the coming night. He hesitated over the rifle; it had proved useless against the ruum, but his military training impelled him to keep the weapon to the last. Still, every pound raised the odds against him in the grueling race he foresaw clearly. Logic told him that military reasoning did not apply to a contest like this; there would be no disgrace in abandoning a worthless rifle. And when weight became really vital, the .30-06 would go. But meanwhile he slung it over one shoulder. The Geiger counter he placed as gently as possible on a flat rock, hardly breaking his stride.

One thing was damned certain. This would be no rabbit run, a blind, panicky flight until exhausted, ending in squealing submission. This would be a fighting retreat, and he'd use every trick of survival he'd learned in his hazard-filled lifetime.

Taking deep, measured breaths, he loped along, watching with shrewd eyes for anything that might be used for his advantage in the weird contest. Luckily the valley was sparsely wooded; in brush or forest his straightaway speed would be almost useless.

Suddenly he came upon a sight that made him pause. It was a point where a huge boulder overhung the trail, and Jim saw possibilities in the situation. He grinned as he remembered a Malay mantrap that had once saved his life. Springing to a hillock, he looked back over the grassy plain. The afternoon sun cast long shadows, but it was easy enough to spot the pursuing ruum, still oozing along on Jim's trail. He watched the thing with painful anxiety. Everything hinged upon this brief survey. He was right! Yes, although at most places the man's trail was neither the only route nor the best one, the ruum dogged the footsteps of his prey. The significance of that fact was immense, but Irwin had no more than twelve minutes to implement the knowledge.

Deliberately dragging his feet, Irwin made a clear trail directly under the boulder. After going past it for about ten yards, he walked backwards in his own prints until just short of the overhang, and then jumped up clear of the track to a point behind the balanced rock.

Whipping out his heavy-duty belt knife, he began to dig, scientifically, but with furious haste, about the base of the boulder. Every few moments, sweating with apprehension and effort, he rammed it with one shoulder. At last, it teetered a little. He had just jammed the knife back into its sheath, and was crouching there, panting, when the ruum rolled into sight over a small ridge on his back trail.

He watched the grey spheroid moving towards him and fought to quiet his sobbing breath. There was no telling what other senses it might bring into play, even though the ruum seemed to prefer just to follow in his prints. But it certainly had a whole battery of instruments at its disposal. He crouched low behind the rock, every nerve a charged wire.

But there was no change of technique by the ruum; seemingly intent on the footprints of its prey, the strange sphere rippled along, passing directly under the great boulder. As it did so, Irwin gave a savage yell, and thrusting his whole muscular weight against the balanced mass, toppled it squarely on the ruum. Five tons of stone fell from a height of twelve feet.

Jim scrambled down. He stood there, staring at the huge lump and shaking his head dazedly. "Fixed that son of a bitch!" he said in a thick voice. He gave the boulder a kick. "Hah! Walt and I might clear a buck or two yet from your little meat market. Maybe this expedition won't be a total loss. Enjoy yourself in hell where you came from!"

Then he leaped back, his eyes wild. The giant rock was shifting! Slowly its five-ton bulk was sliding off the trail, raising a ridge of soil as it grated along. Even as he stared, the boulder tilted, and a grey protuberance appeared under the nearest edge. With a choked cry, Jim Irwin broke into a lurching run.

He ran a full mile down the trail. Then, finally, he stopped and looked back. He could just make out a dark dot moving away from the fallen rock. It progressed as slowly and as regularly and as inexorably as before, and in his direction. Jim sat down heavily, putting his head in his scratched, grimy hands.

But that despairing mood did not last. After all, he had gained a twenty-minute respite. Lying down, trying to relax as much as possible, he took the flat packet of emergency rations from his jacket, and eating quickly but without bolting, disposed of some pemmican, biscuit, and chocolate. A few sips of icy water from a streamlet, and he was almost ready to continue his fantastic struggle. But first he swallowed one of the three benzedrine pills he carried for physical crises. When the ruum was still an estimated ten minutes away, Jim Irwin trotted off, much of his wiry strength back, and fresh courage to counter bone-deep weariness.

After running for fifteen minutes, he came to a sheer face of rock about 30 feet high. The terrain on either side was barely passable, consisting of choked gullies, spiky brush, and knife-edged rocks. If Jim could make the top of this little cliff, the ruum surely would have to detour, a circumstance that might put it many minutes behind him.

He looked up at the sun. Huge and crimson, it was almost touching the horizon. He would have to move fast. Irwin was no rock climber but he did know the fundamentals. Using every crevice, roughness, and minute ledge, he fought his way up the cliff. Somehow—unconsciously—he used that flowing climb of a natural mountaineer, which takes each foothold very briefly as an unstressed pivot point in a series of rhythmic advances.

He had just reached the top when the ruum rolled up to the base of the cliff.

Jim knew very well that he ought to leave at once, taking advantage of the few precious remaining moments of daylight. Every second gained was of tremendous value; but curiosity and hope made him wait. He told himself that the instant his pursuer detoured he would get out of there all the faster. Besides, the thing might even give up and he could sleep right here.

Sleep! His body lusted for it.

But the ruum would not detour. It hesitated only a few seconds at the foot of the barrier. Then a number of knobs opened to extrude metallic wands. One of these, topped with lenses, waved in the air. Jim drew back too late—their uncanny gaze had found him as he lay atop the cliff, peering down. He cursed his idiocy.

Immediately all the wands retracted, and from a different knob a slender rod, blood-red in the setting sun, began to shoot straight up to the man. As he watched, frozen in place, its barbed tip gripped the cliff's edge almost under his nose.

Jim leaped to his feet. Already the rod was shortening as the ruum reabsorbed its shining length. And the leathery sphere was rising off the ground. Swearing loudly, Jim fixed his eyes on the tenacious hook, drawing back one heavy boot.

But experience restrained him. The mighty kick was never launched. He had seen too many rough-and-tumbles lost by an injudicious attempt at the boot. It wouldn't do at all to let any part of his body get within reach of the ruum's superb tools. Instead he seized a length of dry branch, and inserting one end under the metal hook, began to pry.

There was a sputtering flash, white and lacy, and even through the dry wood he felt the potent surge of power that splintered the end. He dropped the smoldering stick with a gasp of pain, and wringing his numb fingers, backed off several steps, full of impotent rage. For a moment he paused, half inclined to run again, but then his upper lip drew back and, snarling, he unslung his rifle. By God! he knew he had been right to lug the damned thing all this way—even if it had beat a tattoo on his ribs. Now he had the ruum right where he wanted it!

Kneeling to steady his aim in the failing light, Jim sighted at the hook and fired. There was a soggy thud as the ruum fell. Jim shouted. The heavy slug had done a lot more than he expected. Not only had it blasted the metal claw loose, but it had smashed a big gap in the cliff's edge. It would be pretty damned hard for the ruum to use that part of the rock again!

He looked down. Sure enough, the ruum was back at the bottom. Jim Irwin grinned. Every time the thing clamped a hook over the bluff, he'd blow that hook loose. There was plenty of ammunition in his pocket and, until the moon rose, bringing a good light for shooting with it, he'd stick the gun's muzzle inches away if necessary. Besides, the thing—whatever it might be—was obviously too intelligent to keep up a hopeless struggle. Sooner or later it would accept the detour. And then, maybe the night would help to hide his trail.

Then—he choked and, for a brief moment, tears came to his eyes. Down below, in the dimness, the squat, phlegmatic spheroid was extruding three hooked rods simultaneously in a fanlike spread. In a perfectly coordinated movement, the rods snagged the cliff's edge at intervals of about four feet.

Jim Irwin whipped the rifle to his shoulder. All right—this was going to be just like rapid-fire for record back at Benning. Only, at Benning, they didn't expect good shooting in the dark!

But the first shot was a bull's-eye, smacking the left-hand hook loose in a puff of rock dust. His second shot did almost as well, knocking the gritty stuff loose so the center barb slipped off. But even as he whirled to level at number three, Jim saw it was hopeless.

The first hook was back in place. No matter how well he shot, at least one rod would always be in position, pulling the ruum to the top.

Jim hung the useless rifle muzzle down from a stunted tree and ran into the deepening dark. The toughening of his body, a process of years, was paying off now. So what? Where was he going? What could he do now? Was there anything that could stop the damned thing behind him?

Then he remembered the dynamite.

Gradually changing his course, the weary man cut back towards his camp by the lake. Overhead the stars brightened, pointing the way. Jim lost all sense of time. He must have eaten as he wobbled along, for he wasn't hungry. Maybe he could eat at the lean-to … no, there wouldn't be time … take a benzedrine pill. No, the pills were all gone and the moon was up and he could hear the ruum close behind. Close.

Quite often phosphorescent eyes peered at him from the underbrush and once, just at dawn, a grizzly whoofed with displeasure at his passage.

Sometime during the night his wife, Cele, stood before him with outstretched arms. "Go away!" he rasped. "Go away! You can make it! It can't chase both of us!" So she turned and ran lightly alongside of him. But when Irwin panted across a tiny glade, Cele faded away into the moonlight and he realized she hadn't been there at all.

Shortly after sunrise Jim Irwin reached the lake. The ruum was close enough for him to hear the dull sounds of its passage. Jim staggered, his eyes closed. He hit himself feebly on the nose, his eyes jerked open and he saw the explosive. The sight of the greasy sticks of dynamite snapped Irwin wide awake.

He forced himself to calmness and carefully considered what to do. Fuse? No. It would be impossible to leave fused dynamite in the trail and time the detonation with the absolute precision he needed. Sweat poured down his body, his clothes were sodden with it. It was hard to think. The explosion *must* be set off from a distance and at the exact moment the ruum was passing over it. But Irwin dared not use a long fuse. The rate of burning was not constant enough. Couldn't calibrate it perfectly with the ruum's advance. Jim Irwin's body sagged all over, his chin sank toward his heaving chest. He jerked his head up, stepped back—and saw the .22 pistol where he had left it in the lean-to.

His sunken eyes flashed.

Moving with frenetic haste, he took the half-filled case, piled all the remaining percussion caps among the loose sticks in a devil's mixture. Weaving out to the trail, he carefully placed box and contents directly on his earlier tracks some twenty yards from a rocky ledge. It was a risk—the stuff might go any time—but that didn't matter. He would far rather be blown to rags than end up living but paralyzed in the ruum's outdoor butcher's stall.

The exhausted Irwin had barely hunched down behind the thin ledge of rock before his inexorable pursuer appeared over a slight rise 500 yards away. Jim scrunched deeper into the hollow, then saw a vertical gap, a narrow crack between rocks. That was it, he thought vaguely. He could sight through the gap at the dynamite and still be shielded from the blast. If it was a shield … when that half-case blew only twenty yards away …

He stretched out on his belly, watching the ruum roll forward. A hammer of exhaustion pounded his ballooning skull. Jesus! When had he slept last? This was the first time he had lain down in hours. Hours? Ha! it was days. His muscles stiffened, locked into throbbing, burning knots. Then he felt the morning sun on his back, soothing, warming, easing … No! If he let go, if he slept now, it was the ruum's macabre collection for Jim Irwin! Stiff fingers tightened around the pistol. He'd stay awake! If he lost—if the ruum survived the blast—there'd still be time to put a bullet through his brain.

He looked down at the sleek pistol, then out at the innocent-seeming booby trap. If he timed this right—and he would—the ruum wouldn't survive. No. He relaxed a little, yielding just a bit to the gently insistent sun. A bird whistled softly somewhere above him and a fish splashed in the lake.

Suddenly he was wrenched to full awareness. Damn! Of all times for a grizzly to come snooping about! With the whole of Irwin's camp ready for greedy looting, a fool bear had to come sniffing around the dynamite! The furred monster smelled carefully at the box, nosed around, rumbled deep displeasure at the alien scent of man. Irwin held his breath. Just a touch would blow a cap. A single cap meant …

The grizzly lifted his head from the box and growled hoarsely. The box was ignored, the offensive odor of man was forgotten. Its feral little eyes focused on a plodding spheroid that was now only forty yards away. Jim Irwin snickered. Until he had met the ruum the grizzly bear of the North American continent was the only thing in the world he had ever feared. And now—why the hell was he so calm about it?—the two terrors of his existence were meeting head on and he was laughing. He shook his head and the great side muscles in his neck hurt abominably. He looked down at his pistol, then out at the dynamite. *These* were the only real things in his world.

About six feet from the bear, the ruum paused. Still in the grip of that almost idiotic detachment, Jim Irwin found himself wondering again what it was, where it had come from. The grizzly arose on its haunches, the embodiment of utter ferocity. Terrible teeth flashed white against red lips. The business-like ruum started to roll past. The bear closed in, roaring. It cuffed at the ruum. A mighty paw, armed with black claws sharper and stronger than scythes, made that cuff. It would have disemboweled a rhinoceros. Irwin cringed as that side-swipe knocked dust from the leathery sphere. The ruum was hurled back several inches. It paused, recovered, and with the same dreadful casualness it rippled on, making a wider circle, ignoring the bear.

But the lord of the woods wasn't settling for any draw. Moving with that incredible agility which has terrified Indians, Spanish, French and Anglo-Americans since the first encounter of any of them with his species, the grizzly whirled, side-stepped beautifully and hugged the ruum. The terrible, shaggy forearms tightened, the slavering jaws champed at the grey surface. Irwin half rose. "Go it!" he croaked. Even as he cheered the clumsy emperor of the wild, Jim thought it was an insane tableau: the village idiot wrestling with a beach ball.

Then silver metal gleamed bright against grey. There was a flash, swift and deadly. The roar of the king abruptly became a whimper, a gurgle and then there was nearly a ton of terror wallowing in death— its throat slashed open. Jim Irwin saw the bloody blade retract into the grey spheroid, leaving a bright red smear on the thing's dusty hide.

And the ruum rolled forward past the giant corpse, implacable, still intent on the man's spoor, his footprints, his pathway. Okay, baby, Jim giggled at the dead grizzly, this is for you, for Cele, for—for lots of poor dumb animals like us—come to, you damned fool, he cursed at himself. And aimed at the dynamite. And very calmly, very carefully, Jim Irwin squeezed the trigger of his pistol.

Briefly, sound first. Then giant hands lifted his body from where he lay, then let go. He came down hard, face in a patch of nettles, but he was sick, he didn't care. He remembered that the birds were quiet. Then there was a fluid thump as something massive struck the grass a few yards away. Then there was quiet.

Irwin lifted his head … all men do in such a case. His body still ached. He lifted sore shoulders and saw … an enormous, smoking crater in the earth. He also saw, a dozen paces away, grey-white because it was covered now with powdered rock, the ruum.

It was under a tall, handsome pine tree. Even as Jim watched, wondering if the ringing in his ears would ever stop, the ruum rolled toward him.

Irwin fumbled for his pistol. It was gone. It had dropped somewhere, out of reach. He wanted to pray, then, but couldn't get properly started. Instead, he kept thinking, idiotically, "My sister Ethel can't spell Nebuchadnezzar and never could. My sister Ethel—"

The ruum was a foot away now, and Jim closed his eyes. He felt cool, metallic fingers touch, grip, lift. His unresisting body was raised several inches, and juggled oddly. Shuddering, he waited for the terrible syringe with its green liquid, seeing the yellow, shrunken face of a lizard with one eyelid a-tremble.

Then, dispassionately, without either roughness or solicitude, the ruum put him back on the ground. When he opened his eyes, some seconds later, the sphere was rolling away. Watching it go, he sobbed dryly.

It seemed a matter of moments only, before he heard the seaplane's engine, and opened his eyes to see Walt Leonard bending over him.

Later, in the plane, 5,000 feet above the valley, Walt grinned suddenly, slapped him on the back, and cried, "Jim, I can get a whirlybird, a four place job! Why, if we can snatch up just a few of those prehistoric lizards and things while the museum keeper's away, it's like you said—the scientists will pay us plenty."

Jim's hollow eyes lit up. "That's the idea," he agreed. Then, bitterly: "I might just as well have stood in bed. Evidently the damned thing didn't want me at all. Maybe it wanted to know what I paid for these pants! Barely touched me, then let go. And how I ran!"

"Yeah," Walt said. "That was damned queer. And after that marathon. I admire your guts, boy." He glanced sideways at Jim Irwin's haggard face. "That night's run cost you plenty. I figure you lost over ten pounds."

The Rats

He cuddled the stock against his shoulder, lined up the ivory bead, and squeezed the trigger. He heard the smack of the hollow-point against wood, and swore, his imprecations echoing hollowly down the dark, empty streets.

Jeffrey Clark expected no reply to his oaths, and got none. The silent village had been evacuated months before because of dangerous radioactivity from the adjoining proving ground for atomic weapons, now also abandoned.

Clark was a physicist, and understood perfectly that the government could not take chances. He knew that present radiation was quite harmless a short distance from the firing range, and there were excellent reasons for remaining here after the jerry-built settlement was evacuated.

In this region, wasteland to begin with, and now forbidden by law, a man would be safe. What enemy, he reasoned, cared to waste a gram of fissionable material on such a locality? Further, when the bombs fell, an eventuality he believed imminent, there would be no panicky mobs to pillage his supplies, menace his life blindly, and, in short, ruin his slender chance for survival.

There was a large store of food in his house, carefully built up during the three-year period when he worked on the proving ground. A small spring provided the only dependable supply of water within hundreds of square miles of desert; the government had left behind dozens of large drums of gasoline, as well as tons of miscellaneous equipment; and Clark was tough enough psychologically to make a good fight of it alone.

The only annoyance—at present, he rated it no higher—was the rats. With the abandonment of the village, they had found themselves short of food. Unable to follow the inhabitants across a pitiless desert, they were in a hopeless predicament. How they had arrived in the first place was a minor mystery to the physicist, but he surmised that a few pairs had been hidden in the huge shipments of material; certainly the once numerous mice, now almost exterminated by their large cousins, had come that way.

In any case, Clark was more interested in their future than their past, for he was finding it difficult to protect his possessions, especially the priceless food, against their inroads.

True, he had the .22 rifle and a large quantity of high-power shells, but the rats were no longer easy targets. Strange as it seemed to him at first, he was convinced they had learned to duck at the flash, like veteran infantrymen. He often bemoaned his blindness in failing to provide rat-traps, but it was too late, now. Any contact with the outer world was definitely taboo. He had no wish either to share his retreat or to be conscripted for the Armageddon which lay a few calendar leaves ahead.

Blowing into the chamber of his gun, Clark returned moodily to the house. Something had to be done. With all his skill, he hadn't shot a rat in days, and the big albino that had just escaped had certainly been a perfect target. And in spite of the food scarcity, they still swarmed in great numbers throughout the town. Either they fed on each other, or else they had learned to catch the ubiquitous lizards that crouched with gently throbbing throats on every sunny surface.

"The question is," he muttered, filling a pipe, "do I concentrate on purely defensive measures, like rat-proofing this house, or take the offensive?" He had repeatedly plugged rat-holes with a mixture of cement and powdered glass, a mortar no rat cared to gnaw for long, but the enemy merely made new passages in the wooden dwelling.

Then, too, a number of minor incidents tended to make Clark uneasy. There was the hole, for example, which he had blocked with a sheet of tin. To his astonishment the rats had managed to strip away the metal, not by haphazard attacks, but through working directly on the tack-heads. Clark was no biologist, but he felt sure such intelligence was uncommon. For a moment he thought, idiotically enough, of a typical professional article: "Observations on an Unusually Adaptable Colony of—" what was the scientific name of the rat, again? "*Mus*" something. As if that mattered, with a world waiting for the assassin's blade. Anyhow, the explanation surely lay in the critical plight of the cunning rodents.

As he sat in the clear white glow of the gasoline lamp, puffing thoughtfully on his briar, a memory of childhood came to him, and he sat bolt upright.

"By George!" he exclaimed. "I should have thought of that sooner. Gramps used to get hundreds that way, out on the farm."

Filled with enthusiasm, he decided to begin at once, although it was late. Living alone, he cared little about clock time, preferring a more flexible, wholly subjective measure.

A brief search located a large, empty barrel, which he sunk in the ground for about two-thirds its depth. This he filled half full of water from the nearby spring. Then, with great care, he adjusted a long plank so that it led ramp-wise from the ground, over the barrel's rim, to a point directly above the water. A few well-placed nails kept the board from moving laterally, while permitting free motion vertically, see-saw fashion. By repeated trials, he arranged the plank so that even a small weight in addition to the bait would destroy the delicate balance, sharply dipping the upper end.

After some moments of self-debate, in which he tried to brighten a dim memory of childhood, he placed several rocks in the water so as to form a tiny island.

Then, with a grunt of satisfaction, he fastened some scraps of food to the high end, and, well pleased, returned to his house.

The moon was shining with that metallic brightness so typical of the clear desert air, and in a highly anticipatory mood Clark seated himself by the window with a 7 x 50 night-glass in his hand. He had not long to wait. Almost immediately he could see through the powerful lenses a group of lithe, furtive forms converging on the barrel with its promise of food. A leading rat, after hesitating briefly on the lower edge of the ramp, crept cautiously towards the top. It had just reached the bait, and was about to attack it with savage hunger, when the balance shifted; the plank dipped in one swift motion, and with a despairing squeak the rodent was plunged into chilly water.

For several moments as it swam about, clawing vainly at the smooth sides and squealing its indignation, the other rats vanished, but when the victim scrambled aboard the rock island and continued to shriek for help, they quickly reassembled, drawn by irresistible curiosity.

To their surprise, the mysterious pathway had returned to its original position, lying invitingly before them. Their natural desire for food was supplemented now by a burning urge to know what was happening to their fellow, still keening loudly, but invisible; and before long a second rodent attempted the incline.

Clark roared with laughter as the board, working with the simple efficiency of perfect design, dropped a second rat into cold water.

Both rats were squealing now, long reedy cries of fear and rage. With diabolical intent, Clark had made the island large enough for only one rat, and a grim battle for possession began.

Excited by the cries, and unable to see what was happening, the free rats returned in hordes, and utterly reckless in their madness, dashed up the treacherous ramp. Only a few held back, among them the large albino, and before dawn Clark's barrel-trap had swallowed fifteen rats, a record it maintained throughout the week.

It was on the tenth day that the situation changed.

Watching through his binoculars, Clark saw a rat hesitate on the lower edge, as usual. Another, close behind, impatiently shouldered by, quickly reaching the top, with its odorous bait. As the first rat still paused irresolutely below, the more daring one actually reached the food, tearing at it ravenously. This sight proved too much for the timid one, and it jealously rushed to join in the feast. With a double-weight towards the top, the plank immediately hurled both animals to a watery death. Clark laughed at this byplay until his sides ached. The rats were so human in their reactions. Or should that be put in reverse, he wondered?

But ten minutes later something happened that wiped the smile from his lips. This time the albino took a hand, remaining calmly on the lower edge while a companion raced up the incline. At the top, the rat tore loose a large fragment of rancid bacon, and beat a nervous retreat. Clark could have sworn the animal looked positively relieved on reaching the ground again.

"Well, I'm damned!" Clark muttered. "Was that intentional or—!"

A few more nights' watching answered that question, and the barrel claimed no more victims.

Although concerned by this setback, Clark was far from beaten. If traps—or at least this type—were futile, there still remained other methods. Poison, for example. An inventory of his supplies, however, proved discouraging. Beyond a small stock of medical drugs, there was not a grain of poison to be had. He made a few tentative trials with ground glass, but found, as a toxicologist had once insisted, that it was nearly harmless.

No, poison in the ordinary sense was out, but death by swallowing didn't necessarily mean chemicals or glass. Clark was thinking of a device often used by Eskimos against bears and foxes. It was simple and effective. You coiled a thin sliver of whalebone into a tight, small spiral, and froze it in a pellet of fat. When an animal swallowed such a lump, it soon thawed out; the deadly coil snapped open, and the sharp-pointed bone pierced the creature's vitals.

Of course, he wouldn't use whalebone, nor was freezing called for. Clark rummaged about in the miscellaneous supplies and found some stiff, springy wire. He cut it into three-inch lengths, which he wound, under heavy tension, to spirals no larger than beans. He made a quantity of such coils, all tied with thread. There wasn't much doubt, he decided, considering what rats ate, that the thread would quickly weaken in their digestive fluids. Then, bingo!

The results were heartening beyond his expectations. Concealed in pills of stale food, or small lumps of flour paste, the murderous spirals soon disposed of several dozen rats, and Clark began to hope that total extinction was possible.

On that score he was soon undeceived. These rats learned with amazing rapidity, and before long the pills moldered away uneaten where he left them.

Meanwhile the creatures were bolder than ever. One night, after filling his dish with food, Clark stepped into the pantry for some salt.

Almost immediately he heard a scuffling noise in the outer room, and feeling certain a rat was after his dinner, sprang out just in time to see a slinking white form slip oil-like under a heavy bookcase. It was the albino again, apparently a leader among the rodents. Clark angrily muscled the massive case aside, and sure enough, a freshly-gnawed passage gaped in the corner behind it. Swearing, he returned to the table, where as he ate, ideas for a new, intensive campaign were mentally marshaled and analyzed.

He was chewing a mouthful thoughtfully before swallowing it when his teeth grated on metal. He paled, fighting sudden almost overwhelming nausea. Then, very carefully, with fingers that shook, he removed from the back of his tongue a shattered pill of hard biscuit. Most of the shell had been stripped off by the action of teeth and moisture, leaving the terrible little spiral plainly visible.

Clark shuddered. But for the accident of teeth meeting metal, the small pellet might have been swallowed. There was no doctor for a hundred miles, and with three inches of sharp wire jammed into stomach or bowels—well, no rat could be more hopelessly doomed.

But that wasn't the point, now. How did the damned thing get on his plate? He had been extremely careful not to leave the tricky pills about. A man living alone learns to take every precaution against accidents of all sorts. Then he remembered the white rat. But that was absurd. Surely it hadn't deliberately dropped the pellet into his food. Rats were adaptable, and these exceptionally so, but this sort of human reasoning was as far beyond them as building a railroad.

When he had recovered his composure, Clark inspected the remaining food minutely, but there were no more spirals. Nevertheless his appetite was gone, and leaving the table, he dropped into a chair, there to puff pensively on a pipe.

"If only I had a cat," he murmured, thinking longingly of the mighty, sandy Tom of his childhood. "Cap'n Kidd would make short work of this lousy vermin."

But it was useless to think of cats; action was called for, and quickly. What he needed, Clark felt, was a large, efficient trap that would shatter the whole rat colony at one blow. After that, cleaning up a few survivors might be possible before rodent fertility made good their losses.

There was a small, sturdy shed a hundred feet from the house, and Clark decided to use that. A careful inspection proved it to be eminently suitable, but just as a precaution, he reinforced it with boards here and there, stopped up a few rat holes, and placed tin sheathing at strategic points.

It was simple enough to build a heavy door that could be released from the house by a cord. He had it slide vertically in oiled grooves, dropping smoothly with great speed. Of course, it was a bit large, but that was no problem, and made inspection of the interior easy.

He wondered about a catch, but concluded no rat in the world could budge the weighty door once it fell. Still, these were remarkable animals, and he ought to play safe. After all, if this trap failed, there wasn't much more to try. An automatic lock was uncalled for, but there was no harm in having a pair of staples at the bottom, and a short stick to engage them. Not that the rats would have time to do much with all that dry wood piled about the shed ready for his match.

When everything was set, he placed a quantity of spoiled food in the shed, and returned to the house. It would take several days, he knew, before the harried rats would enter the suspicious structure freely, but their actual precautions were a revelation. Having succumbed in large numbers to the wire pills, the rats were unbelievably wary. From his window, Clark watched through binoculars, and for three days, as the animals came to the shed in dozens, he marveled at their latest procedure.

Apparently a small group of the rodents were tasters, since before mass feeding began, they scouted the food piles, nibbling everywhere with excellent sampling technique. Only when these potential martyrs remained unharmed for a reasonable period of time, did the main body approach.

But tasters or not, they entered the shed, and by the fifth day in such hordes that Clark felt certain there were few holdouts.

During the late afternoon a week later, therefore, he made his final preparations, replenishing the food, adjusting the cord, and testing the sliding door. He was about to leave, well satisfied, when sudden doubt assailed him. Had he overlooked something? Yes, by George. Suppose the cunning rats had outwitted him by digging a few secret bolt-holes recently. What a fool he'd be, if after all this trouble he fired the locked shed only to have rats pour out of a dozen new holes. True, there was tin along most of the lower wall, and the floor was concrete, but with these rats it was best to make sure.

Stooping, he re-entered the shed, and began a painstaking examination of each metal sheet. While he was fingering the nail-heads, he heard a shuffling noise outside, accompanied by loud squeaks. He smiled sourly. The victims were already gathering for their last feast. The sounds grew louder; they came from the roof, too. He decided to step out and check up. The cord passed through a pulley there, and some rat might jam it—he was in a mood to believe they might do so intentionally, even if that seemed fantastic.

He had taken only one step towards the door, however, when it fell with a crash. Clark stopped in his tracks, swearing angrily. How had that happened? The catch was smooth-working, but still needed a reasonably hard tug on its cord. A hint of panic touched him. Could the rats have done the trapping? No, that was insane. Yet, if they could hold him here for even an hour, with his food unguarded—listen, they were at the door now. Well, he was no damned rat. One yank at the oiled door, and he'd be free. He dug his nails into the rough wood and tugged. The door rose smoothly half an inch, then stopped dead. Perspiration burned his eyes. He exerted all his strength. No dice. It was jammed, all right. He put one eye to a crack, trying to locate the trouble, and saw the great albino just outside. Raging, he peered through several slits before understanding. The short, thick dowel-rod he'd brought to engage the staples was neatly in place. The rats had locked him in. They were all about, and surely there was obscene triumph in their scurryings and squealings.

It was obvious he had completely underestimated them. Yet they had a lot to learn, he thought grimly, regaining his poise. This shed couldn't hold a man very long. He pulled out a heavy pocketknife, hesitated, then returned it, and instead drew the long-barrelled .22 automatic from his belt. A few well placed shots would splinter the door enough to let him reach that dowel-rod. He peered out again to locate the best point, and in the growing gloom saw a bobbing light, then another, and a third. For a moment he thought wonderingly of human aid, but these lights were almost at ground level. Then his heart pounded, and he saw all too plainly. They were rats, each with a flaming stick in its jaws. There was only one explanation now, that was certain. The sticks had been lit at his own gas lamp burning at home, and the motive was horribly clear.

Cursing, half sobbing, he battered frantically at the thick wood. He fired until the gun was empty, but the light slugs only chewed up the door's surface, and in the ensuing silence he heard the crackling flames on three sides.

Abruptly he was calm, and the whole situation seemed humorously ironical as full comprehension came. These were not just highly adaptable rats. Everybody knew that radiation did strange things to living cells, and these creatures had been long exposed. No, they were no more rats than men were apes. These were intelligent, quick-learning mutants, and the huge albino was surely their leader.

Clark felt coolly in his pockets. Yes, a break at last. One bullet left. The heat was stifling; there wasn't much time. He raised the loaded gun to his temple, and above the roaring flames heard a detestable, reedy keening.

At that moment as he stood poised between life and death, there was a flash of light somewhere over the horizon, transient yet so intense the very walls of the shed seemed transparent. The ground quivered faintly, as if a premonitory shiver was running over the world, and far off rumblings sounded threateningly.

Penned up though he was, the physicist understood perfectly. Without being able to see it, he knew the inevitable mushroom was having its brief flowering, tall and sinister, yet a thing of urgent beauty to the dispassionate observer.

Clark sobbed dryly. The raw fiber of his brain was touched with acid. Twice his lips moved soundlessly, stickily, before he said softly, "That was It."

The heat was now utterly unbearable, and even the fate of a world was secondary. He raised his voice to a shout, addressing the squealing mutants outside.

"You out there!" he roared, cringing from the searching flames. "You win, damn you! You may be the only ones left this time next month. It's all yours now. And what the hell will *you* do with it?" Then he squeezed the trigger.

The Fly

Shortly after noon the man unslung his Geiger counter and placed it carefully upon a flat rock by a thick, inviting patch of grass. He listened to the faint, erratic background-ticking for a moment, then snapped off the current. No point in running the battery down just to hear stray cosmic rays and residual radioactivity. So far he'd found nothing potent, not a single trace of workable ore.

Squatting, he unpacked an ample lunch of hard-boiled eggs, bread, fruit, and a thermos of black coffee. He ate hungrily, but with the neat, crumbless manners of an outdoorsman; and when the last bite was gone, stretched out, braced on his elbows, to sip the remaining drops of coffee. It felt mighty good, he thought, to get off your feet after a six-hour hike through rough country.

As he lay there, savoring the strong brew, his gaze suddenly narrowed and became fixed. Right before his eyes, artfully spun between two twigs and a small, mossy boulder, a cunning snare for the unwary spread its threads of wet silver in a network of death. It was the instinctive creation of a master engineer, a nearly perfect logarithmic spiral, stirring gently in a slight updraft.

He studied it curiously, tracing with growing interest the special cable, attached only at the ends, that led from a silk cushion at the web's center up to a crevice in the boulder. He knew that the mistress of this snare must be hidden there, crouching with one hind foot on her primitive telegraph wire and awaiting those welcome vibrations which meant a victim thrashing hopelessly among the sticky threads.

He turned his head and soon found her. Deep in the dark crevice the spider's eyes formed a sinister, jeweled pattern. Yes, she was at home, patiently watchful. It was all very efficient and, in a reflective mood, drowsy from his exertions and a full stomach, he pondered the small miracle before him: how a speck of protoplasm, a mere dot of white nerve-tissue which was a spider's brain, had antedated the mind of Euclid by countless centuries. Spiders are an ancient race; ages before man wrought wonders through his subtle abstractions of points and lines, a spiral not to be distinguished from this one winnowed the breezes of some prehistoric summer.

Then he blinked, his attention once more sharpened. A glowing gem, glistening metallic blue, had planted itself squarely upon the web. As if manipulated by a conjurer, the bluebottle fly had appeared from nowhere. It was an exceptionally fine specimen, he decided, large, perfectly formed, and brilliantly rich in hue.

He eyed the insect wonderingly. Where was the usual panic, the frantic struggling, the shrill, terrified buzzing? It rested there with an odd indifference to restraint that puzzled him.

There was at least one reasonable explanation. The fly might be sick or dying, the prey of parasites. Fungi and the ubiquitous roundworms shattered the ranks of even the most fertile. So unnaturally still was this fly that the spider, wholly unaware of its feathery landing, dreamed on in her shaded lair.

Then, as he watched, the bluebottle, stupidly perverse, gave a single sharp tug; its powerful wings blurred momentarily and a high-pitched buzz sounded. The man sighed, almost tempted to interfere. Not that it mattered how soon the fly betrayed itself. Eventually the spider would have made a routine inspection; and unlike most people, he knew her for a staunch friend of man, a tireless killer of insect pests. It was not for him to steal her dinner and tear her web.

But now, silent and swift, a pea on eight hairy, agile legs, she glided over her swaying net. An age-old tragedy was about to be enacted, and the man waited with pitying interest for the inevitable denouement.

About an inch from her prey, the spider paused briefly, estimating the situation with diamond-bright, soulless eyes. The man knew what would follow. Utterly contemptuous of a mere fly, however large, lacking either sting or fangs, the spider would unhesitatingly close in, swathe the insect with silk, and drag it to her nest in the rock, there to be drained at leisure.

But instead of a fearless attack, the spider edged cautiously nearer. She seemed doubtful, even uneasy. The fly's strange passivity apparently worried her. He saw the needle-pointed mandibles working, ludicrously suggestive of a woman wringing her hands in agonized indecision.

Reluctantly she crept forward. In a moment she would turn about, squirt a preliminary jet of silk over the bluebottle, and by dexterously rotating the fly with her hind legs, wrap it in a gleaming shroud.

And so it appeared, for satisfied with a closer inspection, she forgot her fears and whirled, thrusting her spinnerets towards the motionless insect.

Then the man saw a startling, an incredible thing. There was a metallic flash as a jointed, shining rod stabbed from the fly's head like some fantastic rapier. It licked out with lightning precision, pierced the spider's plump abdomen, and remained extended, forming a terrible link between them.

He gulped, tense with disbelief. A bluebottle fly, a mere lapper of carrion, with an extensible, sucking proboscis! It was impossible. Its tongue is only an absorbing cushion, designed for sponging up liquids. But then was this really a fly after all? Insects often mimic each other and he was no longer familiar with such points. No, a bluebottle is unmistakable; besides, this was a true fly, two wings and everything. Rusty or not, he knew that much.

The spider had stiffened as the queer lance struck home. Now she was rigid, obviously paralyzed. And her swollen abdomen was contracting like a tiny fist as the fly sucked its juices through that slender, pulsating tube.

He peered more closely, raising himself to his knees and longing for a lens. It seemed to his straining gaze as if that gruesome beak came not from the mouth region at all, but through a minute, hatch-like opening between the faceted eyes, with a nearly invisible square door ajar. But that was absurd; it must be the glare, and—ah! Flickering, the rod retracted; there was definitely no such opening now. Apparently the bright sun was playing tricks. The spider stood shriveled, a pitiful husk, still upright on her thin legs.

One thing was certain, he must have this remarkable fly. If not a new species, it was surely very rare. Fortunately it was stuck fast in the web. Killing the spider could not help it. He knew the steely toughness of those elastic strands, each a tight helix filled with superbly tenacious gum. Very few insects, and those only among the strongest, ever tear free. He gingerly extended his thumb and forefinger. Easy now; he had to pull the fly loose without crushing it.

Then he stopped, almost touching the insect, and staring hard. He was uneasy, a little frightened. A brightly-glowing spot, brilliant even in the glaring sunlight, was throbbing on the very tip of the blue abdomen. A reedy, barely audible whine was coming from the trapped insect. He thought momentarily of fireflies, only to dismiss the notion with scorn for his own stupidity. Of course, a firefly is actually a beetle, and this thing was—not that, anyway.

Excited, he reached forward again, but as his plucking fingers approached, the fly rose smoothly in a vertical ascent, lifting a pyramid of taut strands and tearing a gap in the web as easily as a falling stone. The man was alert, however. His cupped hand, nervously swift, snapped over the insect, and he gave a satisfied grunt.

But the captive buzzed in his eager grasp with a furious vitality that appalled him, and he yelped as a searing, slashing pain scalded the sensitive palm. Involuntarily he relaxed his grip. There was a streak of electric blue as his prize soared, glinting in the sun. For an instant he saw that odd glow-worm tail-light, a dazzling spark against the darker sky, then nothing.

He examined the wound, swearing bitterly. It was purple, and already little blisters were forming. There was no sign of a puncture. Evidently the creature had not used its lancet, but merely spurted venom—acid, perhaps—on the skin. Certainly the injury felt very much like a bad burn. Damn and blast! He'd kicked away a real find, an insect probably new to science. With a little more care he might have caught it.

Stiff and vexed, he got sullenly to his feet and repacked the lunch kit. He reached for the Geiger counter, snapped on the current, took one step towards a distant rocky outcrop—and froze. The slight background noise had given way to a veritable roar, an electronic avalanche that could mean only one thing. He stood there, scrutinizing the grassy knoll and shaking his head in profound mystification. Frowning, he put down the counter. As he withdrew his hand, the frantic chatter quickly faded out. He waited, half stooped, a blank look in his eyes. Suddenly they lit with doubting, half-fearful comprehension. Catlike, he stalked the clicking instrument, holding one arm outstretched, gradually advancing the blistered palm.

And the Geiger counter raved anew.

By a Fluke

It is possible to be very intelligent and yet completely helpless—at the mercy of a capricious environment.

For countless generations my short-lived race has contemplated with justifiable bitterness the dominance of a species—they call themselves humans—essentially our mental inferiors, but blessed with a large life-span and superb appendages for the manipulation of matter and energy in a variety of forms.

Because of these two priceless attributes, long life and tool-holding fingers, they rule the Earth, while we can only tune in on a few of their thoughts—many wholly irrational—and fight our joyless, never-ending battle for individual survival.

In the fields of mathematics and philosophy we far surpass these lords of creation, I, myself, after only a fifth of my life had passed, easily solved a number of their most difficult problems in pure mathematics. But without experimental science, our philosophy is sterile; and even our mathematics lacks virility for being out of contact with the laboratory. The brute facts of nature are needed to leaven our metaphysical bread.

It may be futile—in fact, it almost certainly is, for me to squander these last few hours of my all-too-brief existence in reciting the autobiography of one individual of my people; but for the first time we are aware, my fellows and I, of a being able to record this account. We have reason to believe that his instruments are even now receiving and preserving my ordered thoughts.

I spoke of an "account," and yet, in fairness, I will admit that it is more of a protest—a protest, pointless, of course, since nothing can be done, against a world, an evolutionary process, and a fate we find intolerable. Such a protest cannot change anything, but we are sufficiently like the human gods to feel somehow better for it, regardless.

But time is passing all too quickly; I must begin with a personal, yet typical, history. I hope and believe that the being, apparently from some other world, is recording it. One hates to cry aloud to mere emptiness.

My first recollection is that of the dimmest sort of consciousness, wherein I was not yet able to receive the thoughts of my people. It was a kind of suspended animation, which I now know to have been the egg-stage of my life. I seem to remember a rolling, tumbling passage down a twisting tube, through gurgling brownish liquid. That was, of course, a bile duct. Many of my own kind have I sent by that path in weeks past.

I have reason to believe that I left my egg rather quickly; that is a physiological feeling however, and not of great evidential value. Although we adults can receive the young ones' thoughts soon after they hatch, there is no way to estimate, except very approximately, how long they have had to remain in the egg. My own real awareness began when I hatched as a roughly cone-shaped, multicellular, and ciliated mite, a mere blob of living matter.

I was one of the lucky few, born in water. Had I hatched in a dry place, as did so many of my contemporaries, I should not be alive now.

You may wonder how I can know of any events outside my own limited experience. That is the tragedy of the situation: this facility of ours for exchanging thoughts and information. The heritage of the race is readily transmitted to each individual who survives long enough to absorb it. And yet, being without appendages or motility, we cannot implement this knowledge. Nor can we contact the dominant life-form, which might—one cannot be very sure—be willing to aid us. We can listen to many of their thoughts, when the range is not excessive, but they are apparently unable to receive ours. Much of our mathematical information has been acquired in this way. Our conception of their physical world, however, is vague and distorted. I have often wondered just what entities—chemical, electrical, and biological—their mathematics really involves. I can never know. Although I solve easily all varieties of differential equations, including some that have baffled the human experts, it is, for me, a purely formal process, and for that reason less intriguing than problems in the theory of numbers, which most of us prefer. In the latter field, the mathematics is all: no practical relation is implied. With applied analysis, one works in a vacuum. For example, I have solved the problem of n bodies moving in a gravitational field, but have no real feeling for the result.

But I must not digress longer. All that I meant to emphasize is that from the moment I hatched, the helpful thoughts of my elders flooded my consciousness. I knew instinctively what I must do, but the advice I received made the task easier; and above all it alleviated the terrible sensation of facing unique, unknown problems. One was briefed in advance, an enormous advantage.

There I was, a tiny blob of almost naked life, awakening in a strange medium, the liquid humans call water, and feeling within me a burning urgency, a need for rapid fulfillment, with death ticking off the precious seconds. I knew I had to find a certain organism, one that was not too common, and further a creature being hunted by hundreds of my brothers. And my time was limited. *Eight hours*, my advisors told me. *Find It in eight hours, or you die. Swim, little one! Swim hard!* But there was a kind of weariness behind their promptings. They knew how many of us must perish.

I swam, scarcely knowing what I sought; and as I whipped my cilia through the murky fluid, my mentors repeated constantly a description of the animal I needed in order to live. It was a monster compared to me, so big that I might easily fail to perceive it at all except for their promptings. This giant was clad in armor, which I must avoid; it would be wasted energy to assault it there. It was mindless, a mere brute. Men call it a snail, and give it a mouth-filling name: *Lymnea columella*.

I was one of the fortunate few. I found my snail, a colossus grating huge masses of vegetation with a toothed ribbon of a tongue. I was lucky in another way. (It is quite absurd, I realize, to keep repeating the phrase. It is axiomatic among my kind. Only the lucky minority survives; to be alive long enough to have thoughts is to be lucky by definition.) My particular snail held only a few of my fellows. Even as I prepared to force an entrance, I heard the anguished thoughts of forty-three of my contemporaries, who had all unhappily converged on another snail, which was already well-tenanted. The elders warned them, but with the same weary undertone. *If you all penetrate, the host will die, and you will perish with it. Swim away, all who have a little time, and search for another snail.*

They advised in vain. The instinct for survival cannot be checked by intelligence. No one would withdraw, nor could one blame them. As so often happens, they were caught in the time-trap. Each cried that his few hours were up; that there was no other snail near enough. Each apparently hoped the elders were wrong; that somehow the host would live through the mass invasion of its vitals. Or maybe they knew themselves to be doomed and were determined not to let any of their fellows survive. Our life pattern does not make for altruism; one regrets it, intellectually, but fully comprehends the feelings of the individual marked for death and unwilling to meet it in place of his brothers. I heard their last resentful thoughts as the snail died, becoming a poisonous mass of carrion that destroyed my fellows.

I crept over the brute's hard shell until I found soft tissues, and worked my way in. It felt good, almost like being safe in the egg again, with no pressing problems. I found a snug spot in a lymph vessel. There were others of my kind about, but I had enough room. There I settled down to meditate, learn, and await my first change, which the elders informed me would be coming soon. It was during this brief but untroubled period that I mastered many fields of philosophy and mathematics.

After a few hours, my cilia began to drop off, one by one. They were, of course, no longer useful to me, and there was no pain. I became larger, saclike, and dreamy. But my mind was clear, and I learned quickly as the elders drowned my eager receptors with waves of racial information and counsel.

Several more hours raced by, and I began to change. I felt my personality multiplying, and became aware that I was now a collective entity. This made me feel very secure; even if only one of these sub-multiples were to survive the perils ahead, it meant that *I* survived.

There was no exchange of thoughts among us; we were one, and needed no communication.

This odd state did not last long, however. Almost before I realized it, I and my co-descendants were changing again. Each of us became several smaller entities, but still *en rapport* in every way. I myself became six, and shortly thereafter we, all six of us, broke free of the shell of my former body, now a dead thing, and made our way to a different part of the snail. There was much bustle, with many others on the move. But to us, the snail was a world of nearly limitless space, and we had not seriously harmed it. My little group found a pleasant place. On describing it to the elders, they were able to identify it for us as the snail's liver.

At this point in my career, my individuality suddenly returned, and I no longer felt as one with my duplicates, who went about their own, obviously similar, affairs. This was also a brief state, although long enough for me to solve a number of difficult mathematical problems while dreamily sucking nourishing fluid from the spongy mass I clung to so tenaciously. In particular, I verified two famous conjectures of human scholars: that of Goldbach, that every even integer is the sum of two primes; and another of Riemann relating to complex variables.

I had just finished the latter problem, an exhausting exercise when done mentally, by demonstrating to my complete satisfaction that the real part of a certain function was definitely one-half, as the man had conjectured, when I found myself dividing again. It is a feeling one hardly gets used to, especially in so short a life time, and seems to happen with bewildering rapidity as well as too often. By allowing myself to become too absorbed in the last problem, I had missed the usual advance information provided by the elders, but instinct was enough.

In a short time I found myself equipped with a slender vibrile tail and handy suckers at both ends. After a hasty consultation with the elders, I wasted no more valuable moments experimenting with these new organs, but burrowed, rather regretfully, out of my cozy place by the snail's liver, through the soft body into the chilly water.

My instinct, reinforced by a stream of advice from those who had gone before, urged me towards the bank of the little pond. It was a tiresome and unpleasant swim; the tail was not as useful as my earlier cilia; and there were enemies in the water. I saw many of my fellows swallowed up by huge, brainless animals, infinitely smaller than our late host, but gigantic to us, and well-armored. Humans call them water-fleas. I had several narrow escapes myself, as they swim much faster than we do.

It was with a feeling of profound relief that I came to a giant, waving green spear of vegetation on the very edge of the water. The elders cheered me on, saying it was a grass-blade, and just what I needed. I struggled wearily almost to the top.

At this stage my consultants became rather apathetic about my fate, since now, for the first time, one's own effort meant nothing. Everything is a matter of chance from this point on, and there is a kind of anesthetic comfort in that knowledge.

Once more, and quickly, I was transformed, losing my tail and becoming a multiple entity again, protected by a tough, weatherproof shell. This is one of the longer way-stations of our episodic cycle, and I spent many fruitful days on mathematics. It was during this period that I disproved a famous speculation: Fermat's Last Theorem, men call it, which states there are no non-trivial integral solutions of the equation $X^n + Y^n = Z^n$ for n an integer greater than two. I found, oddly enough, and without really expecting to, that there are exactly two prime values of n between 2^{4176} and 2^{4177} for which solutions exist. What a pity that I can't pass this surprising fact along to the human mathematicians, with whom, in spite of their racial arrogance and my bitterness, I feel some kinship of the intellect.

Listening to the comments of my older fellows, I knew what to hope for. Another animal, a really titanic thing, was now necessary for my survival. But it had to seek me out; there was absolutely nothing I could do; my motility was gone.

It was a matter of pure chance that I did survive. I was one of the last of my generation to be saved.

One of the enormous beasts did come by, gulped me down, and parting company with my sub-units, each of which now became a separate personality, I burrowed through the creature's stomach wall and worked my way to its massive liver. Here on this dark bulk, in the flush of my maturity, with hundreds of my companions, I had a magnificent food debauch which now, after almost three months, is just coming to a close.

As both male and female I have poured out eggs and sperm in a single fecund stream for many weeks. Hundreds of my offspring are calling even now from grass blades where they await the toss of nature's coin which will decree life or death.

I have exchanged soaring thoughts with my adult associates, ranging over many an abstruse field of mathematics and philosophy. What a pity this must end! My hold on the shriveled organ is weakening; there is no strength in my anterior sucking disc. Soon I shall pass. This is farewell to whoever is recording my story. If only we had more time, or useful appendages, or even motility, but … no … I …

The above is a record, clarified by the inclusion of certain equivalent names and phrases, of the autobiographical recitation of a strange little organism found by Gobal Denoty on the third planet of the recently discovered system. A study of the writings of the extinct race of bipeds which lately dominated the planet indicates that they were completely unaware of this creature's remarkable mental powers, and listed it merely as a degenerate flatworm, a parasite of sheep: the liver fluke, Fasciola hepatica.

Emergency Operation

The chief surgeon made a crisp, authoritative gesture, and the medical students straightened in their seats. On the TV screen of the auditorium, which covered an entire wall, he was an impressive figure: tall, bony, white-haired, and intensely alive, with time-grooved lines of character on his mobile face. The laughter and conversation died away to an expectant hush. Word had gone around of an unusual case, one that was apparently luring even the senior staff members from their swank offices. As if to emphasize that point, Hoffman and Ball, two major officials of the American College of Surgeons, were walking sedately into the amphitheater to seat themselves among the fourth year students.

The chief surgeon began to speak with the slow, precisely enunciated words of a practiced lecturer. "As you know," he said, "we are confronted today with a rare, but not unique medical problem. The patient, on his way to the operating room right now, suffered a slight abrasion of the left thumb this morning at work."

He paused for a moment, presumably to organize his thoughts, but his hesitation produced an unexpected anticlimax, and many of the younger listeners snickered, taking his remark for humor. Recognizing this reaction, the surgeon frowned.

"No, gentlemen," he said wryly, "I wasn't trying to be funny, however the statement sounded. The point is that this man, dealing with atomics—and rather carelessly, it would appear—rubbed the lesion and managed to contaminate the wound with a tiny particle—less than a ten-thousandth of a milligram, we understand—of plutonium."

There was a sudden nodding of heads among the upper-classmen.

"Normally," the surgeon went on, "a quick, high amputation is indicated, since such a fragment, being highly radioactive, cannot be permitted to enter the main circulatory system. That sounds radical, I know, but it's been our only recourse in the past. The deadliness of this type of isotope, with a long half-life, is almost past belief; the size of the particle is irrelevant. Literally any mass of plutonium, however small, is invariably a killer inside the body.

"In this case, however, the patient was not sufficiently alerted to the dangers of his job, and on going off shift in the afternoon, he was found to be in a dangerous condition. The plutonium had already left his extremity and lodged elsewhere, behaving," he added a little ponderously, "with the typical perverseness of such foreign bodies."

He broke off, stepping aside, so that they could see the large, complex operating table glide in, under automatic control, on its rubberized tracks. It carried the anesthetized body of a burly, middle-aged man. Over the audio system they could hear his faintly whistling breath, typical of the new drug, prontocaine. More intriguing was the rhythmic purr of a pump. A fifty-gallon plastic container of whole blood lay in its metal rack above the patient, and they could see the level fall slowly as the efficient little motor helped his heart drive fresh blood through the man's circulatory system. A plastic tube led from a vein in his right arm to a sump in the tiled floor.

"Yes," the lecturer continued, as if sensing their reaction through the operating room's own smaller screen which kept him in touch with his audience, "the best we can do at the moment is to keep renewing his entire blood supply. In that way, impossible with the ordinary closed circulation, we prevent the corpuscles from being repeatedly irradiated by the plutonium. The excess, which you see being drained off, will be banked and re-processed.

"If you wonder why nothing more positive is being attempted at this time, the explanation is that the particle has lodged in a tiny blood vessel, a capillary, in intimate contact with the posterior part of the optic nerve, where it branches out in the brain.

"Now, if we had two hours, modern techniques of brain surgery would enable us, with every hope of success, to reach that area and remove the foreign body; but the operation is quite difficult, as you professors of anatomy will testify, and in that time, gentlemen, the damage to the optic nerve—it's the right one—and the contiguous brain tissue would be so extensive that blindness of one eye would surely result immediately, to be followed later, as so often happens, by sympathetic atrophy of the left optic nerve, and total loss of sight. The brain lesions would produce less predictable symptoms, but undoubtedly serious ones. A very delicate situation, indeed. Our only hope, therefore, is more rapid action of a sort especially called for in this case. A Geiger counter check has located the plutonium at the point I mentioned; and there being no other alternative, we have sent for a distinguished colleague who is uniquely competent to handle this emergency. It is while awaiting his arrival that I am able to give you this detailed summary of the problem."

There was an outburst of sibilant conversation. Many now guessed what was coming. It was a fortunate medical student who witnessed a case like this one. The last in this school had occurred almost six years earlier, and involved a normally inoperable glioma, one of the deadliest of brain tumors.

As one man the audience stiffened. A glittering speck, like a sunlit mote, was sailing majestically across the dustless, sterile air of the operating room. They could hear a shrill, pulsing beat as of tiny engines. The gleaming dot hovered momentarily, and then swooped down to alight on the stage of a TV microscope. On the auxiliary screen, which came to life immediately, the students saw the magnified image of a metal spheroid. A minute port flickered open, a ramp thrust out, and down this gangway came a microscopic organism. The size and approximate shape of a red blood corpuscle, it moved on dozens of whiplike cilia. Two eye-spots, immense in proportion to the creature's size, glowed symmetrically on each quadrant of the little disc. Lidless and bright, they were aglow with intelligence. A transparent sort of harness made a geometric pattern enclosing the saucer of protoplasm; its webbing held numerous complex instruments.

"Gentlemen," the chief surgeon boomed, "this is one of our newly trained colleagues from Ilkor—Dr. M'lo. He is about to enter the patient's blood stream and remove the particle of plutonium."

A technician came forward with a sparkling hypodermic syringe. They saw the hollow needle, a giant, glittering tube under the microscope, come to rest just before the Ilkorian doctor. A lipless slit at the upper center of the disc seemed to twist in a grimace of comical distaste. One could sense a feeling like that before an unwilling plunge into chilly water. The alien organism wrestled for a moment with the tough surface film at the point of the needle, and noting this difficulty, the technician drew back the plunger a trifle. M'lo was sucked through the opening, and a moment later could be seen swimming nonchalantly about in the clear tonic salt solution of the transparent syringe.

The magnified image vanished from the screen, and the audience saw the technician step alongside the patient. He gave the chief surgeon a questioning glance. "Go ahead, Joel," his superior ordered, and the technician expertly, in a single deft motion, found the great outer vein in the neck which drains the brain itself, and drove the plunger home.

"All we can do now is wait," the surgeon said. "There is no way Dr. M'lo can communicate with us at present. Even under ideal circumstances a very complicated electronic set-up is necessary. But while we're waiting, let me refresh your memories about our Ilkorian allies. As you may recall, it was only thirty years ago, in 1960, that the first organisms from Ilkor, a planet of Procyon, landed on Earth. Luckily our worst period of nationalism was just over, and we made no serious blunders in our treatment of these altogether civilized beings. They are true seekers after knowledge, and before long they made enormously valuable contributions to many phases of our culture. A number of Ilkorians have devoted their best efforts to learning human anatomy and physiology, despite obstacles both in communication and size-differential. This has been accomplished not only through study and consultation, but actual research within the bodies of human volunteers. Being the size of red blood corpuscles and free from bacterial infestation, they make ideal on-the-spot experts in microbiology.

"A few of them—all too few, unfortunately; but they are more interested in theory than practice—have made themselves available as actual medical specialists, aiding in difficult operations. They are in great demand. Dr. M'lo, for example, is kept very busy, so that we were lucky to obtain his services today. He's the one, oddly enough, who in this very room, six years ago, entered the brain of that famous patient and destroyed, in situ, with devices of his own invention, an 'inoperable' tumor. He is an expert on radiation as well as a highly competent student of human physiology, which makes his assistance invaluable in this present emergency. By now, I hope, he is nearing the fragment of plutonium."

This was, in fact, the case. Swimming rapidly through the venous blood stream, battling its current, which while not of arterial strength was considerable, buffeted by corpuscles as bulky as himself, but less solid, Dr. M'lo knew he was getting close. The radiation detector on his webbing had its narrow bubble quivering against the stop. He paused in the rushing flood, annoyed by brittle platelets dashing against him in great numbers. He flailed his cilia vigorously, and huddled against the wall of the vessel where the blood moved more slowly. There was no light from the outside, of course, but to his ultra-sensitive eye-spots every bit of living tissue gave off a faint glow. It was luminescence characteristic of life itself, although far below man's visual threshold and known to him only through the long-neglected researches of Gurwitch.

Just ahead, the vein branched, and it was necessary to take a reading. There was no time to retrace false steps. Every second the plutonium was bombarding the patient's tissues with missiles of tremendous energy and destructiveness. The left branch; no doubt of that. He studied the configuration carefully, drawing on his profound knowledge of human anatomy. Somewhere just a few inches away, there should be a smaller vein, and beyond it the very capillary, nestling against the optic nerve, in which the deadly fragment was wedged, stopped on its journey to the heart. M'lo, however, did not jump to conclusions. No one knew better than he how great were individual differences in the microscopic structure of humans. The major organs seldom varied in their relative locations, but capillary networks were not so obliging. Ah! Here was that last vein, all right. M'lo winced as a shower of nuclei battered his body. He could hear the crackling beat of atomic projectiles impinging on tissue; there was an aura of light ahead, painful to his eyes. He moved forward more slowly, almost with reluctance. What they didn't know, the doctors out there, was the personal agony of an operation like this one. To be sure, he was relatively immune to the worst effects of radioactivity, but the pain was hellish. The lancing electromagnetic rays were like summer sunlight on an inflamed conjunctiva; and a sharp-edged hail of nuclear rubbish, already disintegrated by its passage through tissue and water, pounded his tender body mercilessly.

Suddenly he stopped. A nuisance—a time waster, especially in this narrow capillary, where red corpuscles went single file. Just ahead loomed a white mass, a leucocyte, hurrying no doubt to the aid of the tortured cells, and suspecting somewhere in its vague intelligence a bacterial invasion. Just in advance of M'lo it had slipped through the vessel's wall, and now blocked his path. In its dim consciousness it seemed to recognize him as an alien, with no business in the blood stream. Although he was too big to engulf, it closed in, pseudopodia reaching for him. M'lo had no desire to grapple with the thing, moist, sticky and fetid. His eye-spots were cavities of pain; his whole body cringed under that terrible, relentless rain of atomic bullets. He wanted no more complications. The leucocyte was tenacious and strong, and even though it couldn't easily hurt him, it might immobilize many of his cilia, causing a delay fatal to the patient.

M'lo tried half-heartedly to escape through the cell wall, but he was less plastic than a red corpuscle, and couldn't quite make it at this point in the capillary. Well, there was no more time to waste. With a pair of cilia he whipped a projectile gun from his harness, pressed a stud, and under the thrust of highly compressed argon, a crystalline needle flashed through the plasma to imbed itself in the leucocyte's foamy mass. Instantly the tiny arrow dissolved; it was extremely, but locally, toxic. The white corpuscle knotted itself into an agonized blob. Then its almost invisible membrane burst, spilling loose protoplasm into the rushing fluid. A vacuole collapsed with a faint pop. But by that time, M'lo was on his way again.

The faint aura became a miniature sun; his eye-spots smarted even through the shields he fitted over them. Not too close. Even he couldn't take plutonium at short range. Nasty stuff. He made a quick, expert estimate of the damage; they'd want to know. The optic nerve was badly injured, but not hopelessly. He could see its pale surface right through the translucent capillary wall, itself a mass of lesions. There were drugs that would help those tissues mend. The brain was beyond his observation, but judging from the quantity and hardness of the radiation, there was some chance that the patient would suffer lifelong ataxia. M'lo hoped not.

He took a special grappler from his webbing, unreeling a length of metallic, flexible cord, and swimming as near the fiery, sputtering mass as he dared, sent the device gliding through the luminous fluid, almost at rest here in this far outpost of the circulatory system. It needed several tries, but finally the ingenious claws made a sort of cage about the plutonium, and M'lo pulled the cord tight. His plans were made. There was no time to drag the particle back by the circuitous route he had used in locating it. No, better to haul it away from the optic nerve immediately, and then take the direct, shortest way out.

He swam strongly, tugging at the cord, but the fragment, almost as big as he and incredibly dense, was tightly jammed. Inflammation of the capillary had closed the swollen tissue about it. With a little hiss of annoyance, M'lo snatched a wheeled instrument from his webbing, made a hasty inspection of the vein wall nearest him, and went to work. A few expert slashes with a sturdy knife, and a trio of holes gaped in the tough tissue. In a matter of moments he lashed the device—a simple block-and-tackle unit giving a mechanical advantage of four—in place, and threading the free end of the cord through, gave a savage tug.

There was the sound of ripping cells; the lacerated capillary loosed its grip, and the radioactive lump, sizzling and sparking viciously, was tumbling downstream at him. There was nothing else to do, unless he wanted that red-hot mass to bowl him over. M'lo dropped the cord and fled.

Coldly angry, reproachful of his own blunder, he ducked down a side branch to let the plutonium grate past. He was worried. Suppose the damned thing stuck in a worse place? Ruefully he began to trace it.

Luckily the abandoned pulley was no problem; made of titanium alloy, it would be covered by venous tissue without causing inflammation.

Good! A break at last. He found the particle firmly jammed in another capillary, a minute vessel close by. Only the plutonium's weight and irregularity had diverted it from the main stream; otherwise he might be chasing it through the lungs by now.

Better get out of here. Taking another grappler from his web, he captured the fragment again, made a quick estimate of the situation, and with scalpels in four adjacent cilia, began to slice his way to the skin. The openings he made were too small to bleed; often he managed to slip, corpuscle-like, through a slacker wall of tissue. Only his great strength and dexterity, plus the array of manipulative instruments he carried, made it possible for him to bring the plutonium along. To a man, his task would have compared with that of hauling a loaded boxcar through several miles of tropical jungle. A final slash of the keen blades, and he was out, dragging the radioactive mass after, and standing on the patient's gently heaving chest with a white fold of sterile sheet like a ghastly sky above him.

The watchers saw the technician bend over with a powerful hand microscope, catch the plutonium in a bit of lead wool, and carry it triumphantly away. Beside the almost invisible specialist, waiting wearily on the patient's body, a single tiny spot of crimson welled. It was the only blood shed in the operation.

Story Conference

Even a Martian must eat.

For almost a year now, the Martian had been stranded on Earth, one unhappy alien in a society aggressive beyond all conception of his native planet. Initially he had thought, naively enough, of introducing himself as the first visitor from Mars and accepting graciously the enthusiastic homage of mankind. A better understanding of international affairs changed his mind, which was brilliantly capable. In the present jittery, nationalistic world, hypersensitive even to home-grown dissenters, a lone Martian might easily end up in a Twentieth Century oubliette.

If the Martian had owned one tenth of his father's immense technical knowledge, he might readily have become Earth's foremost engineer, but such background was wholly lacking. When his father's pioneer spaceship had shattered itself in the High Sierras, leaving the young Martian as the only survivor, Fate must have smiled at the irony, for the luckless castaway was that most impractical of all beings, even upon Mars—a poet.

True, his latest work seemed to Martian critics, atrabilious like all their kind, what "Sailing to Byzantium" was to discerning terrestrial literati—a veritable thunderclap of beauty and power; yet to make a living on Earth from poetry was no easier than on Mars. Even the little magazines would have none of it, preferring their own cliques of obscurantist writers.

So for a year the Martian did what he could: namely the backbreaking or menial tasks commonly given by white Americans to dark, by the French to Arabs, and by the Russians to native deviationists.

But for him, all that would soon be past. In his hand at this very moment was a note that could mean salvation. From the minute he had seen the cover of *Thrilling Space*, with its semi-nude girl in the hands of a spidery nightmare whose complexion resembled dirty stucco, the world had brightened. The story's title (how it had shocked even through his imperfect knowledge of English!), "A Martian Castaway," seemed at the time like a personal message of cheer.

For weeks he bought and read avidly the dozen or more publications specializing in science fiction. At first, it was merely diversion from nostalgia and drudgery; but before long, as his quick mind grew perceptive to good writing, he had an inspiration. Surely a person who could write *authentic* science fiction about Mars must necessarily dominate the field. Some fairly mediocre practitioners were reputed to receive five cents a word; he, with his unique knowledge of Martian life, ought to succeed in doubling that figure. It would beat dish-washing hollow.

And now, his first story having been mailed in some weeks ago, he held in one sweating palm a curt editorial note inviting "Mr. Smith" to a conference. Squaring his shoulders, the Martian took a deep breath and knocked gently on the door marked, SOBER SCIENCE FICTION. A few moments later, he was seated opposite a burly, genial man with unruly hair and a knowing eye. The novice waited, filled with pleasant anticipation; maybe he would get fifteen cents a word; the real thing was bound to register among so many phonies.

"Mr. Smith," the editor began warmly, "you have ability. Your story has an excellent plot, action, plenty of suspense, and remarkable, subtle characterization. I like the way you use words in new combinations; like a foreigner almost, but without awkwardness."

The author's melancholy blue eyes brightened. "You liked it?" he asked.

"Yes and no. I couldn't possibly use it."

"I don't understand. You just said—"

"Exactly. It has many good qualities, which I enumerated; but for our readers, it's completely out of the question." He leaned forward impressively. "The people who buy *Sober Science Fiction* are a most select group. They appreciate plot, action, and characterization—in fact, they're connoisseurs of literate writing—but they are absolute fanatics on science. And you, Smith, if I may speak frankly, know nothing whatever about astronomy, biology, or physics." He shook his head sadly. "Why you chose to write in the one field where sound technical knowledge is a *sine qua non*, I can't imagine; but here's a superior style"—he slapped the manuscript for emphasis—"ruined by a comprehensive ignorance of elementary science."

Smith appeared dazed. He fumbled at the neck of his shirt, pale skin oddly flushed. "I've been extremely careful about details," he protested, as the editor raised his eyebrows. "I don't really see where—"

"Obviously not. Details, indeed!" The editor's tone became sympathetic. "That's why I've taken this rather unusual step of explaining in person. You have real talent, and *Sober Science Fiction* is a magazine always on the lookout for promising new writers. Maybe you can be salvaged. I think you can, if you're not allergic to advice."

"You mean," Smith said wryly, "that if my science were—ah—sound, the story would be acceptable?"

"Yes. Although," the editor amended, lips judicially pursed, "I can't give any blanket assurance. I'd want to see such improvement first, naturally."

"I have another story right here. It has details about Mars that—"

"Never mind just now; no time. Let's go over the one you sent in." He riffled the sheets, frowning. "To begin with, here's a planet without water enough to dampen a toothbrush—and you make the hero a crack swimmer! Not only that, but every five minutes he's finding a river, lake, or pond to wallow in. On Mars! Now that's utterly fantastic. Our readers would laugh us off the stands."

"You mean," Smith said slowly, "there's no water on Mars?"

"Oh, Lord! You see? Didn't even bother to look it up, did you? No H. Spencer Jones, no *Conquest of Space* ..."

"But how do they know? Nobody's been there."

"It's getting worse," the editor groaned. "You're even more hopeless on science than I thought. My God, Smith, haven't you ever heard of something called a spectroscope? It's a contraption—no, let's start with a telescope; that's simpler." He raised a cupped fist to one eye, and making a motion as if focusing, peered owlishly at the befuddled writer. "Look," he said in despair; "if there's anything the astronomers are certain of, it's that Mars is drier than—than—" He groped for a suitable comparison. "—than the lead story in last month's *Thrilling Space!*" he concluded, on a note of triumph.

"Well," Smith said with reluctance, "if that's the evidence available, I suppose—"

"That's it. Mars is dry and cold—just as sure as Jane Russell's a mammal! No use questioning well-established facts. Why, even a *Shocking Wonder* reader knows all about Mars. If you pick a planet of Sirius, nobody can gripe even if the natives disport themselves in an ocean of thousand-year-old brandy." He licked his lips.

"Still, one can surely assume—"

"For our readers you can't assume a damned thing. They're all technicians themselves. One of my writers turned out a story about a planet where the atmosphere was a mixture of hydrogen and chlorine gases. With a nice Earth-type sun yet. I'll never know how the hell I let that one by. We got 246 cancellations," he said gloomily. "For a lousy 35 cents some people expect entertainment plus the *Journal of Physical Chemistry*. You know, even the nuclear physics people at Oak Ridge read SSF. Why? Because they get sound science. Okay. Take another point, a biological one this time.

"A few years ago you could make the Martians all purple goo shaped like a topologist's nightmare, with feelers, wings, buck teeth, and living on yttrium metal for choice. That's all passé. The organisms nowadays have to be self-consistent. For example, your hero, Gryzzll Pfrafnik—and say, before I forget: That name. Won't do. Why would a society so far ahead of ours in its technology tolerate such absurd, jaw-breaking names? They'd probably use numbers and/or letters. Call the fellow BT-65-LS/MFT, or something. Scientists like things of that sort. Real systematic. Or if that's too Gernsback for you, there's the modern trend: short, euphonious names of a quasi-American sort. Smit for Smith, C'nor for Connor … and always remember: *Jon*, never John." He paused and looked puzzled. "Sound just the same, don't they? Never thought of it aloud. But remember: *never* use an *h* in Jon."

Smith nodded. "But a people might outgrow the number-letter stage. There are personal, psychological reasons for family names, not just bureaucratic. And if the names have deep cultural and social roots, they may not be changed or replaced by degenerate short forms. But all that's easily rewritten. This biological consistency matter seems to be something else."

"You bet it is. Here's this Pfrafnik—I used to know a delicatessen man with a name nearly as bad as that; nobody could pronounce his either; we called him Max. Anyway, here's Mr. P, 90 per cent anthropomorphic, and what do you do to the poor guy? You give him a completely pointless third eye—and a silly green tentacle. Evolutionarily speaking, that's inexcusable. Why should there be an odd eye between two perfectly good ones, and with the same field of view, particularly in an organism that's obviously meant to be bilaterally symmetrical? What does this third eye accomplish that the other two can't? Bet you never thought of that—just threw in an extra eye and a pretty green tentacle, and hey presto!—there's a Martian. If you looked through a book on comparative anatomy, or read up on the evolution of the vertebrates, you wouldn't make such monumental boners, Smith."

"I thought I explained," the writer objected, his voice a little shrill but painfully precise, "that the third eye was sensitive to infra-red rays."

The editor snorted. "That's even sillier. Dragged in just to make a third eye seem necessary. But it's impossible for such an organ, midway between two normal eyes, to develop a wholly different function while still structurally so similar to its neighbors. If it were on top of his head, like those Sphenodon lizards, or elsewhere on his body—no, even then, our readers wouldn't go for it. Not on such an anthropoid creature."

"There's also a social function for the third eye," Smith protested stubbornly. "It shows great anger. When the girl jilts him, you'll remember, he does a rare thing in giving her the 'third-eye-hate-glance.' Ordinarily it's almost invisible; just a faint whitish line."

"Well, that's a good touch, I admit; but you should work out something with the regular two eyes instead. What I'm trying to say is,

75

keep all those fine bits of characterization; you do very well with some kinds of non-human behavior; but tidy up the astronomy and biology. And drop that damned tentacle."

"It's essential to the plot. You'll recall the social—"

"No." The editor was brusque. "Thirty years ago, they were all right. Every Martian and Venusian had an inalienable right to its full quota of squirming feelers. Not now. One tentacle can ruin a first-class science fiction story; I know, believe me. Why should a handsome, near-human young fellow have one lousy tentacle on his chest? The evolution just doesn't make any sense."

"In the story," said the writer, quivering slightly, "I made it quite clear how, starting from a mutation, the Martians deliberately altered their own biological development. After all, when a race knows enough to modify its own evolution—"

"I merely scanned that part," the editor broke in hastily. "I knew the tentacle would have to go in any case, so I didn't bother with details."

"Was there anything else wrong—with the science?"

"Plenty." He spoke with relish. "But no time for all the boners. You see what I mean. Study science. Get reference books. Check everything—*everything*. Guess only when there's no data, and then be mighty careful. Use good sense. Take that weird sex idea of yours. Two kinds of sex organs on the male, one for producing his own gender, the other for females. An embryologist would die laughing. Cell development simply can't work that way. What we're trying to do, Smith, is outguess the future. Some day we'll land on Mars and Venus. Our descendants will *know* what they're really like. Until then, we speculate—but only and always on the basis of valid, objective, demonstrable fact." He sank back wearily. "I don't think this story can be saved. Try something else, but study up first. Take my advice, and lay off Mars; too many tricky little facts to trip you up. Pick an extra-solar planet they don't know anything about. We get plenty of insane guesses about Mars, but yours is the worst and most careless in all my years of editing. My God! Your heroine's an egg-laying mammal!"

"But you have them here! What about the Platypus? The Echidna?"

The editor gave him a pitying glance. "Sure, the Platypus; I knew you'd bring *that* up. The Platypus is a transitional mammal, low in the scale. Look it up; you don't have to believe me. But a *higher* oviparous mammal is just a pipe-dream—a contradiction in terms. The brain evolves at roughly the same rate as the rest of the organism. A higher egg-laying mammal is just as much of a biological chimera as a cockroach that does algebra. Consistency—you see? Where the devil did you learn such effective English, such convincing behavior patterns without losing your comprehensive ignorance of science—" He broke off in alarm.

"So my science is all wrong!" Smith hissed venomously. "I'm an idiot, am I? Fat lot you know!" He stepped forward, shaking with fury.

"Hey, wait a minute!" the editor gulped. He looked about helplessly. That infernal secretary *would* slip out just now. This bird might get violent. With some of these touchy writers, you never could tell. "There was nothing personal. I didn't mean—" He gaped incredulously at three hard blue eyes blazing ferociously into his own.

"No, nothing personal!" the writer grated. "Me, either!" His shirt front flew open, and a green tentacle shot out, rugose and muscular. Like a snapped whip it flicked the manuscript from the editor's numb fingers.

"A hell of a lot you know about Mars!" Smith jeered. "I was hatched there—out of an egg! Yes, I said 'egg,' you lint-head!" He stepped back. "And another thing; my name is Gryzzll Pfrafnik, and it's no damn funnier than your own. 'Theobald A. Humperdinck, Editor'! What's the *a* for—'Archimedes,' you two-bit scientist? One last remark: on Mars I have a pet cockroach that *can* do algebra; in fact, it does differential equations!" And standing there triumphantly, he awaited the editor's disintegration. Anger dissipated by his outburst, he looked forward with pleasure to spurning all apologies, however abject. Even for 40 cents a word!

For ten seconds there was silence, and for the briefest instant something like confusion flickered in the editor's eyes; then it vanished. He frowned.

"My dear Mr. Pfrafnik," he said coolly, "the oldest excuse of the novice writer is 'But this *really* happened to *me*.' Factuality is no concern of mine, nor of any artist. The question is convincing a reader. You may, sir, *be* just such a Martian as you describe; but your description simply does not arouse suspension of disbelief. Therefore your work fails. And now, if you'll excuse me—" He made an unmistakable gesture towards the door.

And Gryzzll Pfrafnik, the first writer to deal authentically with Mars, slunk out.

The Logic of Rufus Weir

Rufus Weir was calculating on the back of an envelope the number of mice, guinea pigs, hamsters, rabbits and monkeys he had sent to Venus. The total was 246—not including cold-blooded auxiliaries—but he couldn't remember whether that meant 30 mice and 42 hamsters or the reverse. The uncertainty troubled him, because Rufus Weir, Ph.D., M.D., D.Sc.—"our only universal genius in science since Poincaré"—was not used to having doubts, and didn't like the situation.

For example, he was sure that in exactly 6 hours, 18 minutes and 34 seconds the rocket he was occupying (some sentimental technician had scrawled *Marybelle* on its nose, a circumstance which greatly annoyed the doctor) would start its braking action 200 miles above the surface of Venus. He was certain precisely because of those hundreds of laboratory animals which had preceded him on the way. And because he was Dr. Weir.

For ten years, backed by the International Rocket Society, Weir had supervised all the scientific research directed towards attaining the planet Venus. The first small missiles had made barely 500 miles of altitude, and many of their mice had died. But gradually, learning by experience, and using all his talent as a physicist, mathematician, and biologist, he had pushed the rockets higher, made them larger, and secured an increased number of survivors among the rodents privileged (as he would put it in one of his rare facetious moods) to lead even man in this glorious adventure.

Dr. Weir shoved his envelope of computations aside and yawned. He was bored. For weeks he had passed time by solving new problems in the theory of space flight, but even a born mathematician may become stale and detest the most simple and inoffensive symbol of his profession.

In that mood he sought other diversions, even to the point of reciting, with some satisfaction, one of a series of lampoons in verse, directed against him by a skeptical wag who apparently had learned nothing from the V-2's of the '40's through the pilotless moon rocket of 1986. In his dry, unaccented voice, Weir had declaimed to the blank walls:

Listen, my children, and you shall hear
Of the thrilling flight of Dr. Weir:
His takeoff was brilliant; the band played Sousa;
He aimed for Venus but hit Azusa!

Well, he wasn't going to crash in Azusa. In exactly six hours, now, he'd be landing on the second planet, the first terrestrial to do so. Not counting, of course, the mice, rabbits, hamsters, guinea pigs and monkeys. So much for the comical rhymester. What the lay brotherhood of anti-intellectuals didn't realize was the careful smoothing of the way. The constant feed-back, so to speak, giving fresh data for the next tiny advance. Metaphorically, one reached the stars on a path of dead animals.

Even after the first rocket had landed on Venus (Dr. Weir reflected), and without shattering itself—something the earlier ones had failed to achieve—the telemetering devices indicated that not one animal had survived. Promptly Dr. Weir—the medical doctor in this phase—had re-examined the biological aspects of the problem, and instaled new protective equipment designed by the physicist-engineer who shared the same skin. The next missile reported by automatic radio that almost one third of the warm-blooded animals still lived— briefly—and that a few of the hardier creatures, like insects and toads, were nearly normal. On the other hand, the two Capuchin monkeys had gone mad, as indicated by their delta brain waves telemetered back, dying shortly thereafter. All this, of course, without setting foot—paw, rather—on Venus itself.

But there was no reason to despair. One tried again, that's all; mice were plentiful and cheap. From each failure something significant was learned. One by one the loopholes through which disaster crept so insidiously into the silvery projectiles were stopped up; and finally came the joyous day when a rocket not only made a safe landing on Venus, but deposited thereon all but two of its living cargo, and in good health.

It is true, unhappily, that none of the creatures lived more than a few hours; the second planet was inhospitable. Something in the atmosphere, perhaps. Dr. Weir tolerated no perhapses. The pilot-rockets, small and handy, were available in great numbers for just such setbacks. One after another they flamed Venusward, laden with animals to the small bodies of which were fastened highly efficient instruments in communication with the Earth.

The data accumulated slowly, but they were all meaty. Gravitation was rather less on Venus. The air was good enough, although dampish. What killed the mice, then? Answer—after many rockets and a veritable holocaust of the rodent population—hard radiation. Not very penetrating, either; it was merely that these animals were unduly sensitive to that particular wave length. Nothing daunted, Dr. Weir, medical again, prepared serums, vaccines, and even little plastic-lead coats, as if in parody of those stylish garments draped on Pekes and Boston Bulls by the dowagers of Fifth Avenue.

Against such determination, such painstaking, patient, and rigorous application of scientific method, the gremlins of space travel drew back cowed, pondering wistfully, no doubt, on their halcyon days when they had big, vulnerable, bug-filled B-17's to play with instead of an electronic hard nut designed by that terrible, omniscient Dr. Weir, himself as irresistible as any natural force.

The landing of pilot rocket 63 was celebrated by a champagne supper, attended by gleeful officials of the Society. There was many a toast to Rufus Weir, for his telemetering instruments demonstrated beyond cavil that all the animals had survived and gone about the desperate business of making a living on the second planet. It was hoped that a few might last until Weir arrived. To be sure, they were soon lost track of, as batteries ran down, but extrapolation was easy. If a mouse lived ten hours on Venus, so could a man. And if ten hours, why not as many years? So most people would have inferred; even a few scientists, full of champagne, went that far.

But not Dr. Weir. You could almost see the contempt he felt for such reasoning. One doesn't extrapolate (a) mice into men; (b) hours into years—not with his training.

So away went more rockets crammed with monkeys, hamsters, guinea pigs, mice and rabbits. And finally a few chimpanzees, the elite of the laboratory world. When these all prospered—at least until the reports faded out—Weir was willing to admit, provisionally, that The Time Had Come.

As to who should make the first trip, there was nothing to discuss at all. Even though there was no piloting to be done, the whole flight being automatically controlled, the doctor felt disinclined to trust any of his colleagues on the soil of Venus. They were obviously too emotional. The immature chaps would like as not dash off after the first intriguing thing they saw, instead of carefully weighing every action. You had to be level-headed; no room for mistakes, millions of miles from home in an alien environment. Man was no mouse to survive without detailed planning.

No, he would go first, taking enough supplies for six months; and one at a time selected members could follow, each bringing additional equipment to help establish a small colony with facilities for returning, if advisable, a man or two at some later date. He would keep in touch, but he must lead. His pale eyes, wide-set and hypnotic in their conscious intellectual power, stared them down, as always.

"And nobody takes off here until I send word," he ordered.

It took almost five years more to build the first man-carrying rocket, and there was further delay in order to start mass production on those to be used by the other members. Dr. Weir wanted to be sure he would have assistance within six months of reaching his goal; and only when rockets were ready to come off the production line did he blast free, nearly six years after the first animals had landed safely on Venus.

And now, directly underneath, the cloud-wrapped planet awaited its first man. Abandoning his retrospection, Dr. Weir breathed a little sigh of satisfaction—not that he'd had any fears—when, right on time, the braking jets vibrated his ship. Slowly the big rocket decelerated, falling through the fleecy clouds. In a moment he would see the surface, something no Earthly astronomer had ever done.

But even a cold-blooded, level-headed person may be excused for wondering at the sight of a city with oddly human overtones in its structures.

Dr. Weir stepped from the ship, took a few tentative breaths and, systematic as ever, tested his respiration, blood-pressure and anti-radiation buffer concentration, deliberately keeping his thoughts undistracted by speculations about the city a few miles from his landing place. It was only after recording all these dial readings in his neat notebook that he looked up and saw Them.

A five-foot mouse came forward on large but still dainty paws, followed by a six-foot hamster, a seven-foot rabbit, and a chimpanzee the size of Goliath.

"Remarkable," said Rufus Weir, the dispassionate, his brilliant mind carrying out with ENIAC rapidity a series of logical inferences from the living data before him. "Obviously," he stated aloud, "the animals that survived, reacting to a lesser gravity and assorted radiation, have mutated and evolved with unusual speed, aided, one presumes, by a brief gestation period. I wonder if that's because my buffer loses its potency after some months? I'll have to be sure to keep myself well-injected."

"You needn't bother," the chimpanzee muttered in a hoarse, thickly accented voice. "You won't be here long."

"I believe you spoke!" Dr. Weir said, his tones only a trifle strident. He studied his dials again. "Not a hallucination; my brain waves are completely normal." He rubbed his big nose. "This isn't quite so obvious a problem: why English?"

"It is our opinion," a six-foot rabbit, grey with brown splotches, said in a polite voice, "that human language, mostly English, heard by so many of our ancestors in your laboratories and elsewhere, was impressed upon their brains and germ plasm in such a fashion that after a high rate of mutation, when communication was inevitable, our synapses chose the line of least resistance. Our evolution made language necessary, and so we drew on our racial storehouse for the only one we had experienced." After this peroration it took a deep breath.

The scientist gave the animal a sharp glance. "That is utter nonsense," he said crisply. "You imply the inheritance of acquired characters, a theory which, as every child knows, is completely discredited. Go back and read even Muller."

The rabbit retreated, visibly abashed. "Well, anyway we talk English," it muttered doggedly.

"Don't argue with him," the chimpanzee snapped. "Before you know it, he'll be giving *us* orders!"

"Naturally," Dr. Weir agreed, eyeing him coldly. "It is the duty of the best brains to give direction to society. Anything else retards the development of civilization." He looked at the rabbit again, which refused to meet his gaze. "Just as another point, your explanation has a logical hiatus miles wide. The animals that heard English never lived long enough to transmit anything; they were mostly small rodents with brief life-spans."

"No," the ape said bitterly. "Not here. No more condescension, please. You and your organization slaughtered hundreds of my ancestors and theirs." He gestured towards the growing crowd of animals.

"Without malice," Weir replied, showing his disgust for such emotional thinking. "There is no room for malice in science. Your people—I don't believe it's correct to refer to all of them as ancestors—died in the interest of humanity so that Venus might be conquered. Nobody hated them; no unnecessary cruelties were practiced."

"Precisely," said a blue-green hamster the size of a pony, its nose quivering. "We bear no malice either. Nobody hates you, and there will be no needless cruelty."

"But if you plan to kill me—?"

"We don't plan any such thing," the chimpanzee retorted, shocked. "In fact, we fervently hope you'll live. You've done as much for my ances—er, people. It's just that you arrived most opportunely. Our first long-range rocket, designed for Mars, has been held up for want of the proper laboratory animal. Everything possible will be done to insure your survival—on Mars, of course. But don't accuse us of malice: that's unreasonable, and it hurts."

Dr. Weir bowed slightly, a gesture reverting to his student days at New Gottingen.

"The logic of your position is unassailable," he said gravely.

"Bon voyage," they replied, equally courteous, leading him to the waiting missile …

Unfortunately the flight sponsored by the Venerian Rocket Society of Mice, Hamsters, Rabbits, Guinea Pigs, Monkeys and Apes was a failure, blowing up almost half a million miles from Mars.

But the animals were not disheartened. They knew the value of persistence; and as long as they could send terse, provocative messages in Dr. Weir's name, they were assured of fresh specimens for experimental use—direct from the eager ranks of the International Rocket Society—every month. But just to play it safe, they asked, on the pretense that female technicians were needed, for a few competent women, receiving a choice lot recruited by the terrestrial organization, and not long out of the science classes of Vassar, Bryn Mawr, Connecticut College and similar sources of feminine scholarship.

It is sad to report that none of his colleagues (chosen naturally from those not reserved for breeding) showed the same admirable objectivity as Dr. Weir. Many, in fact, displayed rather childish signs of resentment at finding themselves re-routed to Mars, with passage not guaranteed.

The Entity

The emissary from a distant planet was addressing the World Council in closed session.

It was a super-secret conference. Only the assembled senior statesmen knew of the visitor's presence on Earth; and at the moment it was all they did know, except that he bore a message of immense significance for humanity. It was a strange experience for the members, since the emissary's essential nature was incomprehensible to their minds.

One instant the Council saw a glinting, cloudy mass the size of a man, and the next—a tiny pillar of bluish haze. There were times when they heard strains of atonal music and felt pulsating colors. And always they had an odd, not unpleasant visceral awareness.

But they felt little strain, for the visitor's motives, still to be explained, were obviously benevolent. From the moment he had taken over their public address system, speaking in a baritone voice of bright, unearthly beauty, the terrestrials knew him intuitively for a friend.

When the brief excitement attendant upon this first contact with another planet had subsided, the emissary began his message. After a few preliminary remarks to create the necessary empathy, he said, with humorous apology in his tones: "Now I will tell you a little story. It leads to a decision you must make soon. And I offer my services to implement that decision, if necessary.

"I hope to make the account simple, clarifying as much as possible the problem you face. If you can imagine yourselves trying to explain to a completely alien intelligence—that of a mantis, for example—the physiological effects upon its species of DDT, you will understand something of my task and excuse any obscurities. The basic situation, I believe, will be quite clear."

He didn't stress the enormous mental gap between mantids and man, with its obvious parallel to his own role. But that was only courtesy, they knew, and they accepted the fact without resentment.

"Several million years ago," the emissary continued, "when I was still in the learning stage—" Here he sensed their shock and his voice seemed to smile a little sadly. "It's an incredible age to you, of course, a point not irrelevant to the problem ahead. But more on that later.

"I was at the time curator of a sort of zoo which we maintained on a nearby planet. We had combed the galaxy for specimens, and possessed a great variety of life-forms whose countless divergences were of constant interest to science. There were living crystals, gases that waxed philosophical, electromagnetic intellects, and a host of other beings even more foreign to your experience.

"We were, I confess, rather smug in holding that no really different creatures could possibly exist. After all, we had collected for ages, the last truly novel organism having been captured long before.

"Then we were disillusioned. A scoutship sent in an emergency report that a life-form was passing through our solar system; and purely as a routine gesture, I went out to inspect it. Naturally I expected the thing to be a duplicate, basically, of some specimen already in our custody. To my astonishment, it was altogether new, and of a complexity that surprised me.

"Nor do I mean—and this is not vanity—that the entity was in any way superior to my own class of beings. It is true that we pursued it in vain for many months, unable to cope with the thing; but neither was it capable of harming us. We are equally complex, but fundamentally different.

"None of the ordinary methods enabled us to seize it. Traction rays, force patterns, space warps—nothing seemed able to constrain this creature. It passed easily through all kinds of matter, was immune to our excellent arsenal of traps, and coexisted in a multitude of dimensions more numerous even than our own.

"In short, it would have escaped almost effortlessly, when luck came to our aid. One of our best scientists, at work in a laboratory outpost some light years away, saw the entity pass, with my fleet of ships in futile attendance. He had just finished some experiments on a device which I shall call the T-ray, a subatomic manifold outside of your experience or imagination. Four of his little ships had grouped themselves to generate a tetrahedral pattern with the new ray, and we were amazed to see the specimen hurl itself against that structure without the slightest penetration.

"Naturally, I took prompt advantage of so fortunate a circumstance. The four laboratory ships, under my orders, stopped their generators, and by a superior bit of maneuvering reformed the tetrahedron about the life-form. It was a neatly sprung trap, and a most successful coup. In spite of its utmost efforts, the thing was helpless, and we bore it home in triumph.

"I see you are confused, unable to relate this rather verbose account to Earthly affairs. Please be patient. It is vitally necessary to prepare your minds for an important revelation.

"Now, as curator, I called upon our most capable scientists to make a thorough study of the alien being, which they did, taking well over a thousand years of your time. There was much we found out, and more that remained baffling. We were unable, for example, to determine its method of absorbing or utilizing energy; and some phases of its physical structure seemed mutually contradictory. Nor were we able to communicate with it by any means whatsoever.

"Although we searched thousands of stars and planets for other specimens, we found none of its fellows; and yet we had reason to believe ours was only an immature individual of the species. The implication was inescapable that the entity came from some part of space too distant even for our ships to explore. We now believe that it originated at the farthest edge of the universe.

"Millions of years passed, but there remained a large residuum of knowledge we were unable to master. Certain aspects of our captive were as puzzling then as in the first weeks of its capture. I might point out that we never retain specimens which genuinely wish to be free; but in those days we erred occasionally in assuming that an organism's mere inability to communicate in our terms meant satisfaction with life in the zoo. The offer I mean to make shortly is a violation of that humane code, but justifiably so.

"To return, however, our study of the strange creature came to an abrupt end. Because of a careless technician, the force pattern was momentarily disrupted, and moving with tremendous velocity, the prisoner escaped. Of course, we pursued it; but our T-ray ships were no longer conveniently grouped, and before we could get organized, the entity was many light years away, hopelessly beyond tracing. Its speed, now that it had apparently matured, even in captivity, far exceeded that of our best scouts.

"But we did not abandon the chase. While not of the first priority, the recapture of that specimen was one object of every exploratory expedition. As we ranged farther into space in our systematic mapping of the galaxy, we found many remarkable beings, but nothing so different as our former prisoner.

"And then, not many centuries ago, our scouts reached this solar system of yours. Long before seeing the planet's disc, they knew from instruments that the entity was here. This was its chosen home. Immediately word was flashed back, and we sent scientists to survey the situation.

"There was, to begin with, the question of whether or not to leave the thing in its picked environment for most effective study. It is often more fruitful to examine a life-form in its own setting. And that, generally speaking, is still the problem: to leave it here or take it back with us. As you will see, the matter is of profound concern to humanity.

"But do not be alarmed. The decision will be yours entirely. I am only trying to supply the needed background for your debate on the question.

"It was possible for us to reconstruct much of the thing's history after its escape from our zoo. There were long periods, we believe, when it paused motionless in the void. And there were times when it traveled at enormous velocity, pervasive yet unified, tenuous but concentrated. It might have ended its journeying at any one of countless planets, but chance or the working of subtle instinct brought it finally to a medium-sized star with nine newborn worlds.

"One of these—your Earth—seemed suitable, and in its fashion the entity settled on and through the steaming globe, racked with earthquakes, scoured by abrasive tides, and seared by chemical vapors. It lapped itself about the tortured planet to wait with the patience of a billion years' perspective.

"And the inevitable happened. A cloudy speck of heavy, unstable molecules, a near virus, stirred to life under the fierce actinic rays of the youthful sun, ending the entity's long vigil. It must have eaten soon after, appreciatively, but with circumspection. With food its hunger grew, and as the ages passed, each living thing knew this alien and paid it toll, early or late."

Here the emissary paused, and they were aware of his pity.

"Remember that the entity was and is utterly imperceptible to the crude senses of its victims, although a gifted few among the higher animals vaguely felt at times its sinister imminence.

"So it was natural that when man arose to become Earth's only naming creature, he called this being after the sole evidence of its presence, never dreaming it was native neither to the world nor man, but sprung uniquely from some galaxy on the rim of the universe.

"It is here now—today—inside and outside the Earth, permeating every molecule with hyper-dimensional tendrils. I can see in this room that one of you—no, I didn't mean that." He stopped, and there was a tense silence.

"Of all living things," he resumed hastily, "only the most primitive, recalling racially what had awaited those first colloidal blobs in the warm sea, learned to resist, even in part, the entity's pressing demands. Over these—the protozoa—it has but limited power.

"We—my people—could still tear the entity's fibers from the Earth; but in millions of years its presence here has had a profound effect upon life. Evolution—what a tortured mechanism that has become on this planet! The terrible swell of 'natural' increase—a wholly abnormal development, really—is just one example. Nowhere else are things like that. Your problem is indeed one of bewildering magnitude.

"I know that most of you are beginning to understand the nature of this dilemma and its implications for mankind. If I remove the entity, now that your world is conditioned to geometric increase, the result could be catastrophic indeed: a gigantic compost of organisms in one writhing mass. The living devouring the living, so that the fragments, still alive, become somehow part of the devourer.

"The decision must be yours and yours alone.

"Say, then, men of the Council, will you live forever, knowing the consequences of such a choice?

"Shall we free you from this alien elemental—this entity you call Death?"

Whirlpool

"In there, accursed scientist!"

His mind numb, conscious only of the thundering agony in his head, Joel Craima reeled through the doorway. Standing erect on sheer nerve, he managed to focus his gaze on the leader of the group.

"Hull!" he grated thickly. "You—why—?"

"Yes, Hull," said the black-robed giant, his deep-set eyes burning with fanatic fire. "Once I helped run this hellish plant. Now I'm going to atone by destroying it. God and the Good Earth!"

"So you're a Jay Dee! Hull—a damned Jay Dee!" Craima put his hands to his ballooning head and looked about in dull wonder. They were in a metal-walled, windowless room. In the center of the concrete floor was a huge drain, into which four large pipes discharged gurgling streams of dirty, steaming water.

Craima recognized the set-up. This was a sump-room of one of the Atomic Power Plants.

A robed figure muttered something to Hull, and Craima returned his wandering gaze to the renegade. Once Nat Hull had been a top scientist on the A.E.C., and look at him now, dressed in one of those silly sackcloth robes. But then he always had been a little queer, with strange bouts of near-hysteria occasionally.

"Not necessary," Hull answered his subordinate, with a glance at Joel. "When this plant blows, he'll go too."

Craima stiffened. "What do you mean—blows? What are you up to, you crazy Jay Dee?"

"Yes, I am a Judgement Day Saint," Hull said calmly. "The Saints have known for a long time what must be done, but they lacked the technical skill to do it. Now I'm supplying that. In a few moments I intend to disconnect the tell-tale circuits and force the neutron channel switch past the infinity stop. You know, I imagine, what that means."

"You can't do such a thing!" Joel cried incredulously. "For God's sake, man—if this plant blows, it'll take the Earth with it! Do you know how many tons of osmium beta have been added since you—"

"We're aware of all that," Hull broke in contemptuously. "You seem to forget that the Judgement Day Saints have been inspired to wipe the Earth clean of all this Godless science. If the Lord sees fit to destroy us all utterly and begin anew, that is His will. If He chooses a few to survive, even as Noah, blessed be the Lord!"

Staring at the man in dismay, Craima wondered if he were dreaming. If not, Hull was surely mad.

"You're insane," he snapped. "Before this reaction reaches a critical stage, there'll be a Commissioner here with the Emergency Crew."

Hull stolidly shook his head. "Put no trust in material things," he said in sepulchral tones. "Repent before it is too late. We have slain the other two Commissioners. The Lord is striking through us, His servants. You are alive only because we needed you to open the Main Gate. Even if the Emergency Crew were summoned, they would not have time to force the gate. And, besides, who is to call them? With the signaling system disconnected, no distress message can go out. No, Joel, I advise you to make your peace with God. We are locking you in. My brethren and I will pray for you when our work is done." He glanced keenly about the room, and herding his followers out, slammed the heavy door. Craima heard the lock snick home. Then silence.

With a muttered curse, Craima struck his fist against the steel panel. Nursing the stinging knuckles, he tried to organize his thoughts. There was one ace in the hole, thank heaven. Buried under the skin of his forearm was a tiny, flat Bell Transmitter. By its aid he could readily contact the one technical crew on duty. Although his brother officials were dead, Joel knew that the Main Gate, which opened automatically only to the personal and particular body radiations of a Commissioner, could be forced, given enough time.

But time—that was the crucial problem. There were two Atomic Power Plants, one in each hemisphere. *Which was he in?* If he called the crew to the wrong one, they'd never find out their error until the other plant blew. Breaking down the huge bank-vault door was a difficult task; they'd have to torch and blast through. They wouldn't have enough time left to tackle the other plant after a false start. If only the Bell Transmitter were directional …

Damn a complacent government that kept one lousy Emergency Crew on duty. If he could have them scare up another relief gang, and send one to each plant—no, not enough time.

There was a faint, purring rumble in the bowels of the building, and Craima groaned. The deadly switch had been thrown. He fought against a feeling of panic. Earth had been criminally careless. For years the two giant plants had automatically poured their mighty streams of power around the world with only the most casual inspections. Three Commissioners and one Emergency Crew were responsible for the whole works. The servo-mechanisms were just too dependable, that was the trouble. Now two of the key officials were dead and the third a helpless prisoner. He'd been neatly slugged and brought here unconscious so that his body radiations would open the Main Gate and admit the fanatic crew.

A search of his pockets revealed nothing of use. Even his small pocket-knife had been removed by Hull.

There could be no escape from the room, that was certain. It was up to the transmitter. But he must know which plant he was in. How could he tell here in this windowless room, bare except for the sucking drain whose gurgles seemed to mock his helplessness?

Joel began to hammer on the steel door with his fists. If he could lure Hull back, he might be able to trick him into giving the vital information. Not knowing of the transmitter—it had been installed long after Hull left the Commission, and was a jealously-guarded secret of the A.E.C.—he would have no reason to hide his knowledge of the plant's location.

But repeated pounding brought no response. Doubtless the fanatics were off in some corner praying. It was plain, Joel thought sourly, that Hull expected to be a modern-day Noah. He gulped. One thing was certain, even if Hull got fooled, that wouldn't help anybody else. He thought of his own wife, Marcia, and perspiration beaded his forehead. Better to do anything—even the wrong thing—than nothing. An axiom of the military.

He couldn't stall any longer. A decision had to be made. He placed a finger on the flat box he could feel under the skin of his forearm, and began to press out the code. "Emergency Crew— Attention! Proceed to—" He groaned. Which plant? Alpha in the northern hemisphere? Beta in the southern?

He stared blankly at the sucking whirlpool of dirty water, trying to take the gamble that had all humanity for a stake. Little bits of varicolored matter spun madly in the current as they passed down the drain. The flow was beginning to slacken, another unpleasant omen. The whirlpool chuckled.

Suddenly Craima stiffened, and a light seemed to flare in his tired brain. With trembling fingers he completed the message: "Proceed to Plant Alpha. Bring equipment CD-47 and full emergency supplies—"

The sweating crew had just flung themselves panting on the cool floor. Craima, a wet cloth about his aching head, sat wearily upon a converter. He gazed ironically, but with obvious satisfaction, at the black-robed men lamenting under the guard of a husky youngster wearing the neat, green uniform of the World Constabulary.

"You certainly cut it fine," the foreman reproved Joel, with a grin. "But considering your fancy headwork, we'll call it square. And how you happened to think of it, I can't imagine. I know my engineering, but—" He shrugged.

"It was simple enough, once I got on the right track," Craima replied. "Elementary physics, but a sort of by-path. I damn near forgot to remember it! But when I saw that stuff in the water making pretty clockwise spirals as it went down the drain, the light dawned. Only in the northern hemisphere does water go down a vertical drain spinning clockwise."

Smiling, he added: "Look it up yourself, Irv—or try it on your own washbasin."

The Unwilling Professor

On that fateful afternoon Fatty Schultz and Irv Lece had cut their last classes, and were taking a gloomy walk together, scrambling through the scrubby brush well behind the athletic field.

There were good reasons for their unhappiness. Fatty was failing in Calculus II with a velocity that varied directly as the square of the number of lectures attended. Irv's math instructor had informed *him*, with a kind of loathing respect, that his only salvation lay in recommencing the study of arithmetic—taking five or ten years in the process—and then retiring to a cave for perhaps another fifteen in the vain hope of digesting, through meditation and prayer, the multiplication table. After that, Irv might be ready for elementary algebra, but not, the professor hoped to a merciful God, in this unfortunate institution of higher learning.

As a matter of fact, the whole of their fraternity, Omega Pi Upsilon (usually referred to on campus as "Oh P-Yu") was in the same boat regarding almost every subject offered at Bateman College. Bateman had courses that ranged from Aardvark Breeding to Zythum Brewing, but no field of knowledge troubled them more than mathematics.

Hence the long face on Irv Lece. Fatty's visage also strove to elongate, but simply wasn't built for such an accomplishment. Instead, his piggy little eyes, ordinarily glowing with a kind of coarse good-humor, were now smoldering with resentment.

They had just seated themselves in a small clearing, where Fatty, after setting his calculus text on a grassy mound, began to heave rocks at it, when there was a whistling scream, a jarring *whump*, and before their bulging eyes a small disc lay crumpled, barely ten yards away.

A shrill creaking came from this odd craft, which looked like a manhole-cover some eight feet in diameter and twenty inches thick. Then, as they stared in wonder, a badly-sprung port opened crazily, and a small rabbit flopped out. It may be stated here that the creature was not actually a rabbit, but that any difference between the disc's pilot and an ordinary cottontail was imperceptible to the naked eye.

For a moment the rabbit swayed drunkenly, its big eyes cloudy, then it hopped towards Fatty, preferring, perhaps, his larger gravitational field over Irv's. Extending one snowy paw, it squeaked: "Good afternoon, gentlemen. Permit me to introduce myself. I am a good-will ambassador from Venus, and by your conventions should be addressed as 'Professor.' My name," he added a trifle pompously, "is Iglowt P. Slakmak, and I hold degrees comparable to your PhD, LLD, and M.D." All this in a very British accent.

Fatty gave a hoarse croak; Irv's knees knocked together.

"Come," the rabbit chirped, "chin up, fellows! There's nothing to be afraid of. I speak English because we've been monitoring your radio broadcasts for years. Television is a bit trickier, but we've seen a few. And by listening to educational programs, I've learned a great deal about terrestrial culture, which I notice is based upon cigarettes, used cars—but never mind that, now. I must get to Washington and present myself. A rival of mine is about to contact Mars for the first time, and I hope to send in my report on Earth first." He peered at them anxiously. "You do understand me, chaps, don't you? I learned the best English from the B.B.C., you know."

Seeing that the two boys were still dumb, the rabbit, with a mighty effort, picked up the three-pound calculus text, which was bound in a revolting green. As he did so, a paper fluttered out, and the professor deftly scooped it up. He studied Fatty's messy scrawlings for a moment, then said warmly: "Ah, I observe that you chaps are beginning the study of elementary mathematics." He shook a paw waggishly. "The limits are wrong on this integration: they should go from pi-over-two to pi-over-three first, instead of to zero. There's a discontinuity at pi-over-three, and your result, that the center of gravity of this six-inch cube is nine feet to the right, looks somewhat implausible."

At this, Fatty finally found his voice. "A discontinuity?" he gulped. "Whassat?"

"Aw, you know," Irv rebuked him. "Old Cusp's been gassing about 'em for days, now."

"Has he? Well, what is it, if you're so smart?"

"I don't remember," Irv said brazenly, "but at least I heard the name before."

"At pi-over-three," the rabbit broke in with authority, "the denominator of the integrand vanishes. To put it loosely, the function becomes infinite."

Fatty looked at Irv; Irv gaped at fatty. The piggy eyes lit up. "A rabbit that knows math!" Fatty breathed.

"Knows it! He wrote the damn book—a real brain!" Irv exulted.

Once again their eyes met meaningly. "You always said," Irv remarked in an abstracted manner, "that you could lick the guy who invented calc."

"I sure can," Fatty asserted, "but—" He paused; then with a speed surprising in one of his bulk, his thick hands shot out, and Professor Slakmak, the eminent Venusian savant, found himself dangling by the ears from stubby, freckled fingers. He kicked with a vigor shockingly undignified.

"Let me down!" he squeaked furiously. "This is outrageous. A friendly ambassador's person is sacred among all civilized peoples; your national President shall hear of this insult!"

Fatty looked at him, showing uneven teeth in a loose grin. "Bugs Bunny," he gloated, "you are now the official mascot of Omega Pi Upsilon!"

"I second the motion," Irv said, shuffling in excitement.

"We'd better hide his ship, though," Fatty cried, full of ingenious intelligence now that nobody was grading him for it.

"It's too big, ain't it?" Irv replied doubtfully. "Simmer down, you!" he ordered the writhing professor. "We don't wanna choke you, but—" The captive subsided, contenting himself with little quivers of indignation.

"It's awful light," Fatty muttered, shoving the damaged saucer with one size eleven shoe. "We'll move it over here, pile a lot of brush on top, and—"

"—Start a fire!" Irv interrupted joyously.

The professor gave a piercing squeal of protest.

"No, stupid," Fatty told him, winking. "If the prof here helps us out this semester, we'll give him back his old disc, right?"

"Right," Irv agreed, crossing two fingers.

In fifteen minutes, even with Fatty working one-handed, the ship vanished under a pile of stiff brush. "That's that," Irv said, taking a deep breath. "Now—"

"We can't take him like this," Fatty remarked, swinging the professor by his ears and giving him a shake by way of emphasis.

"Why not? We just been rabbit-hunting, that's all."

"Too risky. Even if the professor keeps quiet, some joker from another frat might get nosy."

"He'll be quiet," Irv said grimly. "I know how to hit a rabbit on the neck with the edge of my hand—" Here the professor began to kick frantically, and Fatty snatched his hind legs, holding him rigid from ears to toes.

"There's an old cardboard box back there," Fatty said. "That'll do the trick."

A few seconds later the sullen captive was stuffed unceremoniously into a damp, moldy container, and the two students returned to the campus, their hearts free from mathematical worries.

"The frat will owe us plenty for this," Fatty said darkly. "We've never had anybody to coach us in math."

"They'll be licking our boots," Irv agreed. "But they always have, the poor dopes!"

That night the professor, poorly refreshed by some wilted carrot tops and water, found himself in a circle of eager Omega Pi Upsilon's, delivering a detailed lecture—mostly problem-solving—on Section 45 of Broota's "Introduction to the Elementary Rudiments of the Differential and Integral Calculus."

He was a good teacher, and when either his enthusiasm or expository art faltered, Fatty revived it quickly with a sharp pinch or stinging slap. So, although the average I.Q. of the fraternity was seventy-six, a certain amount of mathematics got through; and it was almost midnight before the unhappy ambassador found himself lying in a dirty, fetid cage, formerly the residence of the fraternity parrot, who had expired for lack of intelligent dialogue to copy. Rabbits, even Venusian ones, cannot weep, but the professor's soul was heavy within him.

And so it went, day after day, week after week.

"I am quite amazed," Professor Cusp told a skeptical colleague towards the end of the term, "at the remarkable way Schultz and his Oh P-Yu bunch have improved. Their homework these last six weeks has been excellent."

"Somebody's coaching them—or doing it outright," was the cynical reply. "I find no improvement in their zoology."

"No, that's what I suspected at first, but it can't be true. For example, on last week's extra credit problem—a real stinker—they turned in over a dozen correct solutions, all different. Nobody would go to that much trouble for the P-Yu crowd; they're about as popular on campus as Malenkov is with the D.A.R."

Another colleague, who had been listening, demanded: "But you won't let Fatty Schultz by, will you?"

"I'll have to," Cusp admitted. "Even though his exams are still horrible, I give quite a bit of weight to good homework, so—"

"You swine!" the other said sourly. "Now I'll get him."

Cusp laughed. "Ah, but you're supposed to be tough; they're afraid of you."

"They'd better be. It's a pity the biology lab has to experiment on poor chimps while we give degrees to anthropoids like Fatty!"

That night Fatty told his unwilling mascot the bad news. "I'm sorry, Prof," he said genially. "It's only one more term, then I'll be done with math, and you can go back to your disc. But my last course is with old Totient, and he's rough."

"You promised!" the professor squealed angrily.

"This time I mean it, honest."

"Hey, Fatty," a fraternity brother objected, "ain't you gonna leave the prof to our gang? Just cause *you're* through—" He broke off in confusion as Irv kicked his ankle, hard.

"Ignore the jerk," Lece reassured the crestfallen rabbit. "When Fatty and I finish our math requirement, you're on your own again. Course, you'll have to promise not to tell the President!" Over the professor's head he winked broadly at his friends.

"I won't do it! It's a cad's trick!" The rabbit's brown eyes were bright with rage.

Fatty pawed his soft fur with one lardy hand. "C'mon, Prof, be a sport," he urged, greasily affectionate. "We like you a lot. You wouldn't let us down now."

"I—will—not—do—it! You promised—"

"You will, too!" Irv grunted. "Don't give us any backtalk. If I have to twist your ears—"

"Use the cigarette lighter," somebody suggested, half ashamed. "He's only bluffing again."

"I'm not," the professor said sturdily. "You can burn me, kill me, but I won't tutor this bunch of cretins any more!"

"Where does he get those words?" a student wondered aloud. "What's a cretin?"

"Irv," Fatty said in a sly, buttery voice, "where's that nasty pooch who adopted the Delts last week? The one that chased the chaplain into Tom Paine Hall. I'll bet he's a first class abbitray oundhay."

"Mac," Irv addressed a slender, dark boy, "they keep him in that shed by the athletic field. Go and—ah, borrow him, will you?" Mac left.

"What's an abbitray oundhay?" the professor quavered.

"You'll find out!" Fatty told him grimly. "Don't they teach pig-latin on Venus?"

There was a strained silence, while some members of the group whispered protests. But there was no open resistance. Fatty and Irv ran Omega Pi Upsilon with an iron hand.

Then the door opened, and Mac, tugging hard at the collar of a large dog, lurched into the room. "Here's Hotspur," he grinned, as the brute strove to mangle the cowering professor.

Hotspur was a canine melting pot. The Spitz in his ancestry seemed to predominate, but there were plain traces of Airedale, Setter—and crowning evidence of some mis-alliance—Dachshund. White teeth bared in a slavering snarl, the dog glared at the rabbit, lunging against his collar as Mac held hard.

But the professor had collapsed, all his courage gone. "A dog!" he gasped in horror, and Hotspur seemed startled at the human voice emerging from a rabbit. A thin whimper came from the professor. "Take that monster away," he begged. "I'll do anything—anything!"

"That's better," Fatty chortled. "But we need this good ol' hound more than the Delts do. Put him down in the basement—just in case." He eyed the professor, who shrank into a furry, abject heap.

"My new prof, Dr. Totient, is tough," Fatty said. "Bugs Bunny here is gonna have plenty to do. We'll clear out now and let him prepare his assignments! See that you watch those signs," he jibed, handing out what he had so long received. He fastened the rabbit's chain to its stout staple in the wall. "Here." He fished an apple core from his jeans, and tossed it at the professor, giving him an oily smirk. "Just to show there's no hard feeling. Eat hearty!" He stumped out, followed by his companions.

Gradually it grew dark, and the deserted fraternity-house was quiet. Ravenous, the professor finally nerved himself to nibble the apple core, which to his sensitive nostrils reeked of Fatty. He had just downed the last noisome fragment, when there was a loud, inquisitive sniff at the door. He grew rigid. Another sniff and the shoulder thrust of a heavy body.

Insecurely shut, the door swung open, and a huge, white form stalked in. The professor cringed, moaning a little, the hot alien scent of dog in his nose, prepared to meet a terrible death.

"Ssst!" the big mongrel admonished him. "I'm a friend," he rumbled in slow, thick English. Trotting over, he took the slender chain in his great teeth, and threw his thirty-pound body into the wrench. The staple pulled free.

"Let's get t'hell out of here," he grunted, "while your bunch is gone."

"B-but my ship," the professor stammered, staring in bewilderment. "It's broken down, and those two awful boys will find me before I can fix it."

"Never mind; I'll give you a lift in mine. I'm heading for Washington, then I'll have to report back on Mars. I can drop you either place. I just got word myself, only a few days ago, that our two planets had finally made contact. They asked me to find out where you'd disappeared to, but I never dreamed you were here. When I heard you talking English—! But we'd better scoot. I've spied out this place long enough—I don't think it's quite representative."

They had just reached the brush behind the library, where the professor's passionate story was completed, when Hotspur, looking back, saw lights flash in the fraternity house windows.

"Wait here," he said cryptically. "Be right back." He sprang into the brush, and vanished. A few moments later, the anxious professor heard some yells of agony coming from the campus, and before long Hotspur returned, panting.

"I know you'll get a sympathetic hearing in Washington," he gasped; "and we Martians abhor violence, but there are times—" He rubbed one paw against his mouth. "I didn't like the taste of Irv, but Fatty's even worse! I hope," he added viciously, "they have to take Pasteur treatments!"

"Me too!" Professor Slakmak agreed cheerfully. "And best of all, they'll flunk math—but good! Where's your ship—pal?"

Guilty as Charged

His hand on a dial, Manton turned to Kramer, ready with the video-audio tape recorder.

"All set, Dave?" he asked, a slight hum in his voice.

"Okay," Kramer replied, ostentatiously cool. The tape began to unwind with whispery precision, and Manton faced the screen, now beginning to glow. Shadowy images flitted across it, gradually sharpening to familiar shapes.

It was too bad, Manton felt, that he had been forced to choose a single small region of space-time on which to focus; the restriction was very annoying. But the field equations did indicate an additional range of about forty feet straight ahead, obtainable by varying a particular input factor. And even with all these limitations, the basic calculations had required months of expensive time on one of the fastest electronic brains available.

It had been something of a problem, too, deciding what unique setting should be computed. Manton believed that his conclusion was a logical one. Obviously, there was no point in going too far ahead; the limited view on the screen might seem chaotic—everything new and different, with few ties to his own day. Nor would it be reasonable to look forward a mere fifty years. One couldn't expect really significant changes in so brief a period. About 225 years, he decided, was probably best—not that the machine would hit it on the nose, anyway. And on that basis the months of brain-twisting mathematics, the design of thousands of electronic units, and the hair-splitting calibration of a dozen complex servomechanisms, had all been undertaken and successfully completed.

Gratified as he was, Manton couldn't help feeling a little disappointment. He had focused on the heart of this city in Massachusetts, hoping to capture the image of some busy public place: a scene sure to convey the maximum information about the mores of 2181. It was rather a let-down, then, to find himself viewing what was obviously a mere courtroom. True it was a magnificent, soaring chamber, with countless fascinating innovations of a minor sort, which he planned to study later; but Manton feared that two centuries and a quarter could not have seen any vast changes in English common law, already hallowed by time.

There would be new crimes, no doubt, either political or related to novel, intricate technologies; and a humane, streamlined, efficient courtroom procedure. Certainly, one would look in vain for either a Jeffreys or a Darrow in this enlightened age. The former would not be tolerated; and the latter would not be needed. Yet a court of law would not have changed to the extent, for example, of transportation, communication, or recreation, just to mention a few categories of human activity.

It was with mixed feelings, therefore, that he watched the two-foot-square, glowing screen, less interested at first in the trial itself than in the triumph of his genius, and the people, with their odd clothing, so loose and light, and their vigorous, almost beefy, bodies that radiated health.

There was a huge, illuminated clock calendar just at the border of his field of view; it gave him a glad thrill to see the date: April 14, 2183. He wrenched his eyes away for a brief glance at Kramer. Dave pointed to the calendar and grinned.

"Missed it by only a couple years," he said. "Nice work."

"Lucky," Manton grunted. "Plain lucky." He turned back to the screen.

Just beyond the calendar, against the same wall, was a sort of bulletin board, giving data about the case being tried. Manton could read "State vs. Frances Wills," but the next line, which presumably named the charge, was out of focus. And the machine had no leeway laterally. Too bad, but the proceedings themselves ought to clear up that point soon enough. He should be able to tell a murder case from a trial for bigamy, even in pantomime.

Now, as he watched, the accused was seating herself with obvious reluctance in the flowing contours of a witness chair. She had something about her, Manton thought, an air of strange vitality, perhaps. She was not young, about fifty, he guessed, although it occurred to him that anybody who looked only fifty in 2183 was more likely pushing ninety. Even in his day, the visible signs of senescence had been thrust ahead a decade or more within a few years.

The jurors filed in; apparently the court had been in recess. He noted that there were fifteen, and snorted. Fifteen-twelfths more chance (he couldn't help thinking mathematically) for illogical verdicts, if this bunch retained anything in common with 1956 juries. Still, they were not a bad looking group, really. Nine men and six women, of middle age mostly, but with three boys and two elderly ladies for balance.

There was the judge. Not much difference in his case. Portly, grave, and seemingly a bear for dignity. No robe. Thank God they'd given up that absurd hangover. Odd; no spectators either. A change for the better; they often put improper pressure on jurymen, just as the papers did. The judge's eyes, Manton noted, redeemed him. They were caverns of melancholy compassion. A jurist who found no perverted pleasure in sentencing social misfits had much to recommend him in Manton's opinion. But then, the cynical thought came, for whom was the compassion? Maybe the judge had ulcers—or were they finally licked after more than two centuries? He doubted it.

It was most unfortunate that he couldn't read lips; understanding this trial was not going to be so easy after all. The prosecuting attorney, a youngish man, with a surprisingly round, good-humored face, was addressing the jury, pointing now and then at the defendant. Although he seemed not unsympathetic to her, she glared at him with alarming malice. She must be, Manton concluded, a vindictive old harridan indeed. You'd think that after so many years the principles of psychiatry would have made such social unfortunates very rare. This one probably owned a fire-trap tenement; she looked the type. No, there wouldn't be tenements in 2183; it must be a more enlightened age than that. A clean courtroom proved something. Public buildings are always cleaned and modernized last. Those even in the biggest cities in his own day: Chicago, New York—why, prison was hardly more depressing than the courtrooms.

Although he knew little enough about law, Manton felt sure that procedures had changed greatly. Witnesses were seated facing the accused, for example. Most of them were restrained, but one woman, with a ravaged, unhappy face, got quite emotional, even waving before the jury a photograph, a wonderful, three-dimensional one, he noted with interest, apparently of a young girl. Later, she tried to attack the prisoner, but guards smoothly intervened. The prosecutor, looking like a chubby, brooding child, helped calm her, but she spat like an angry cat towards the accused, who merely gave her repeated, sidelong glances, half malicious, half contemptuous.

"Whistler's mother," Dave said, pointing at the defendant. "Poisonous old biddy."

Manton pulled his gaze from the bright square, a little annoyed at the comment. He liked to be judicial.

"Lucky you're not on the jury," he said evenly.

The defense attorney, tall and casual, seemed to have very little part in the trial, except for an occasional unemphatic objection. Manton guessed his case had been presented earlier, and that this was the prosecutor's second and last summation. There was an air of fait accompli about the case; it seemed that the defense was merely a routine gesture.

But it was by no means clear just what crime the old woman had committed. Apparently she had offended a number of people, for several of the witnesses showed dislike of a personal nature. There was even a touch of comedy—or so Manton accounted it, although nobody present seemed amused—when one old man, a very shaky and garrulous individual, displayed a photograph of a magnificent prime steer. As a former farm boy, Manton gasped at the meaty perfection of the animal. The old man pointed to the likeness, and shed senile tears; once he shook a trembling fist at the old woman, and the jury looked grave. The foreman slammed his right fist into his left palm, nodding vigorously; one of the old women pursed her lips disapprovingly.

Manton shook his head, running one hand through the rusty hair. He peered at Kramer, who raised one eyebrow comically. What possible connection was there between a steer, for example, and the other picture, that of the young girl? Was this grim old lady a cattle rustler, and had that old man and the girl owned a prize beef? Manton thought of his own 4-H days and grinned wryly. He'd have been damned annoyed if anybody had stolen his own blue-ribbon steer. Absurd idea, though. If there were one crime most unlikely in her case and considering the date, it was cattle rustling. As well expect shipwreckers in 1956 Cornwall. And what about that boy with the withered arm? What was his grievance? He had pointed to it repeatedly, contrasting it with his sturdy left arm, and showing, in vivid pantomime, how the atrophy had progressed from fingertips to shoulder.

Ah! Was this it? The old woman was guilty of reckless driving; poor reflexes, no doubt. In some high-speed vehicle of the age, she had crippled the boy, killed the steer—and as for the girl of the picture, she was killed, too. She was the boy's sister; they had been leading the steer down a highway—no, it was all speculation.

And what about the last witness? The gloomy fellow who had shown pictures of a ruined house. The structure lay in a heap as if dynamited; and the man indicated with a kind of melancholy satisfaction, how all the neighboring houses, so similar in their architecture, were unharmed. How did that fit in? Manton gave Kramer a puzzled glance.

"Blows up people's houses, too," Kramer said, shaking his head in reproof. "I told you she wasn't nice."

They were still speculating, when the trial was recessed. Here was a chance to tinker with the input factor and focus ahead a few more feet. Manton felt a glow of pleasure as saw the foreground fade out, while the courtroom's farthest wall became clear as coated glass to the probing beam.

At the extreme fifty-foot range, just past the courtroom itself, was a chamber he found very intriguing. It was lined with light, hospital-like wall-tile, and housed but a single object: a small, metal hut. The door to this was open; and inside he could see a wheeled table of the sort employed by surgeons, except that the flat top was uncushioned and had eight-inch walls on every edge. There were straps, and yet it could not be for operations; if the person were to lie on, or rather in, that box-like table top, the walls of the metal hut would almost touch him on every side. There was certainly no room for a surgeon at all, and anyway this was not a medical center but a hall of justice.

Manton flashed back to the courtroom, finding that the recess was over. To his surprise, some attendants had wheeled in a great, complex instrument, not unlike the smaller electronic calculators he was so familiar with. But it was not one of those; no question about that. He could read some of the large dials. There was one for blood pressure, another for temperature, and many more marked with terms beyond his comprehension: Rh, Albumin, Ph, Sigma Coefficient, Curie Potential, and Dubos Count. This machine was rolled alongside the witness chair.

Manton stared. It was evident that the device was to be used somehow on the defendant, and that she resented the idea. Only after several husky guards seized her lean wrists, ankles, and shoulders, did the struggling woman submit. Moistened contact plates were fastened to her arms and forehead. Needles were deftly inserted into her leathery skin. She writhed, raving, her lips flecked with foam. The jury shrank from her feral glares. As the burly attendants held her immobile, a specialist flicked various controls on the machine. He manipulated them with bored familiarity; apparently it was an old story to him. Dial needles quivered, and the jury, much concerned, discussed their significance.

Most of these readings meant nothing to Manton, but he did wonder about two of them. The old woman's temperature seemed to be impossibly high: 115 degrees. Even he knew it ought to be near ninety-eight, and that she was well and strong, outwardly, at least, with a fever that should have been fatal. And her pulse, that was only forty, and should have been about seventy. The woman was a freak of nature, if he understood even those few readings.

Whatever the machine indicated, its findings had a decisive effect upon the trial. The defense attorney had been weak enough, and this seemed to finish him. Evidently the old woman's guilt was beyond question, although why sickness was a crime, Manton couldn't imagine.

"That contraption finished her," Kramer muttered, stooping over his camera to adjust the focus. "But just what in hell—?" His voice died away in a querulous mumble.

Certainly the jury had no doubts; their verdict, delivered without leaving the courtroom, took only moments. The judge's pronouncement was equally brief. Now, Manton expected, she would be taken to some cell block beyond the range of the machine, and the courtroom cleared. He leaned forward, almost touching the screen, as the same attendants dragged her not to incarceration, but rather to the mysterious little room he had inspected earlier.

Kramer uttered an impatient sound, and Manton straightened up, aware he was blocking the electronic camera which was recording the trial on tape.

"We'd better shift to the other room," he said. "There's something funny going on."

He refocused in haste, just in time to see the old woman, fighting with insensate fury, being strapped to the table, which stood just outside the little hut. Was this some legal, anti-crime treatment? Something to cure the accused's criminal illness?

And now a white-coated man, obviously a doctor, came in, as did the judge and jury foreman, the latter looking particularly queasy. At a nod from the judge, the doctor prepared a hypodermic, and as the helpless woman squirmed and gibbered, made an injection directly into a vein of her arm. In a matter of moments she relaxed, but her eyes still glared hate, and only after a second injection did they close.

Could this be an execution? No, her breast still rose and fell; she was only unconscious. But maybe she would die soon. Manton gulped, tempted to switch off the machine. He had no stomach for such things. Yet a hypodermic of morphine was a great improvement over the gallows or gas chamber. Such a method would be worthy of 2183. That is, assuming there was any excuse for a death penalty, something hardly acceptable even today.

But why were they wheeling the table and its contents into the metal hut? If she were to die, why not in the open? Was it some quirk of 22nd Century psychology?

An attendant shut the door and twirled a locking wheel. The little group drew back. The judge looked meaningly at the foreman, whose face was dead white. Then the former made a slight, imperious gesture, and one man, moving to the far wall, threw a big knife-switch.

Manton started as the massive contact points arced in a flash of lacy white. Heart thumping, he saw the spectators wait in silence for thirty seconds. Then, at a nod from the judge, the attendant opened the switch; and the foreman, taking a deep breath, advanced to the metal hut. With a hand that shook violently he turned the wheel; the door swung open, and Manton's stomach snapped itself into a sick knot. He heard Kramer draw in a single hissing breath. There on the table, still smoking, was a heap of dirty grey ashes, almost filling the box-like top.

No misinterpretation was possible. It was a monstrous act. The old woman, murderess perhaps, very likely insane, but a fellow human, had been anesthetized—thank God for so much mercy—and burned to ashes in an electric incinerator. Was this the humanitarian climax of over two hundred years more of civilization?

Kramer was swearing in a monotone, and automatically, without comprehension, Manton followed, with the machine, the execution party's return to the courtroom. It was empty now except for an elderly porter. He was just altering the big bulletin board, and as he shifted it slightly, Manton was able to read the words which had been out of focus during the trial, together with some others added moments before:

STATE vs. FRANCES WILLS
CHARGE: WITCHCRAFT
VERDICT: GUILTY AS CHARGED
PENALTY: DEATH BY FIRE

The Mannering Report

The third report was competent but dull: an involved statistical analysis of the comparative efficiency losses suffered by steam and electric power plants during the last decade. It re-affirmed the symptoms of the peculiar disease without suggesting either a cause or a cure.

Only a few specialists listened with attention; most of the audience were eagerly awaiting report number four, traditionally the focal point of each session, and, in this instance, an object of persistent, fantastic rumors.

Dr. Matison, the chairman, after leading polite applause for the speaker, stepped to the lectern. An immediate hush fell over the group, and the tail-end of somebody's emphatic complaint: "—doesn't know a damned thing about topology!" boomed across the silent hall as if shouted.

"Gentlemen," Matison announced in his dry, incisive voice, "the next report will be made by proxy, Professor Raymond having been chosen to deliver it." He waited for the brief murmur of comment to subside, and added: "It is a communication from Sir Walter Mannering."

Despite his upraised hand, their initial gasp was succeeded by a strident babble. Such a reaction was hardly remarkable in the circumstances, for Mannering, a titan of mathematical physics, had mysteriously vanished more than thirty years earlier, in 2138.

Finally, after several chaotic moments, the scientists settled down in charged silence as Professor Raymond came forward with a slender manuscript.

"Gentlemen," he said, "a few words of preliminary explanation are in order. The original of this report, written on a crude variety of paper, and carefully preserved in a box of copper alloy, was found only last week in the course of archeological excavations in France. Comparison of the writing with samples in our own files has established beyond any doubt that Mannering is the author.

"The first few sentences explain what happened to him, why the box turned up in France, and how long it has awaited discovery. The existence of many similar communications is indicated later, and search for them is already under way."

He moved to the lectern, opened the manuscript, and in a clear, resonant voice began to read:

"The year is approximately 112,846 B.C., as estimated from the stars; the place, Paris, or rather where that city will be eventually. It is not the purpose of this paper to chronicle my daily experiences in prehistoric France—some of that has been done in previous reports—but rather to supply evidence for a most significant fact of cosmology.

"It will suffice to say that in 2138, while vacationing in France, I had the misfortune to pass through a species of discontinuity commonly labeled a 'time warp.' Although the existence of such anomalies has long been established mathematically, nobody else, to my knowledge, has ever had such an experience. Whether other disappearances can be so explained, I leave to later discussion; neither will I consider such provocative questions as 'Is this world actually an earlier state of "my" world, or one of infinitely many alternates?' I must necessarily assume the former hypothesis. The possibility that I may later discover my own reports is another matter for speculation, but not now. My fifth report, incidentally, gives a new mathematical approach to space time singularities.

"It is now almost 28 years since I arrived in the 1,129th Century B.C. from the 22nd Century A.D. This report, which I intend to seal in a metal box like the preceding thirty-two, draws heavily on a journal started almost immediately on my arrival. (Such is the conditioned response of a man trained in science.) At first, I used my own notebook and pencils; later, of course, I had to improvise fresh writing material. The bulk of my journal, which I discontinued two years ago, comprises report number thirty.

"To repeat a statement not altogether relevant to this particular communication, but which is part of the overlapping technique used as a precaution against serious gaps in the record, I found a primitive nomad society scratching out a marginal livelihood here in France. It was instantly apparent that if my exile was to prove tolerable to me and fruitful for future generations, I must not delay in achieving physical and moral supremacy over my quasi-human neighbors. Without such an ascendancy, my life would have been in constant danger; my fellow men are cannibals, to whom any outsider is food.

"To a competent scientist the problem of over-awing savages is hardly a challenging one. No doubt that even my small repertory of magic tricks would have served; but a few basic missile weapons easily sealed the victory. I add, parenthetically, that my bow and sling were never permitted in the hands of any other individual; rather they have been kept in the realm of things tabu, and all meddling with them severely discouraged. I do not wish to have on my conscience any improvements in the art of killing; humanity has more than enough talent for that without my prompting. It may be argued that the bow, for example, by its merit as a hunting device, would quickly augment the food supply, and so raise the standard of living. But I preferred to attempt that objective through agriculture, the domestication of animals, and above all, *power*.

"There you have the heart of my program. History, I believe, shows that the chief obstacle to man's conquest of his environment has been lack of power. This is not to minimize the importance of good agricultural practice, but that, too, is closely linked with farm machinery.

"Man's first giant step in this direction was undoubtedly the domestication of the horse or some similar quadruped. This—team and plough—must have multiplied the food supply tenfold.

"But that was not my starting point. Real progress, I felt, depended upon the prompt harnessing of steam, the genie of the Industrial Revolution. It was a task more congenial to one of my training than the capture and breaking of shaggy little ponies.

"I shall not recount in detail the events leading to my complete disillusionment with the first phase of this highly ambitious project. That will be found in my eighth report. Unless I wished to tackle single-handed the prodigious task of creating from the crudest raw materials a modern power plant, however modest, it was essential to train a corps of assistants. Remembering how in my own day the few unspoiled natives of Africa and South America had readily acquired the subtle techniques of laboratory science, I was quite hopeful about the feasibility of a training program. In my capacity as witch-doctor—for that is surely the proper term—of local tribes, I undertook the education of some forty children, ranging in age from six to fourteen years, so far as this could be estimated. I assumed without much reflection that young children could be trained as easily in prehistoric France as twentieth century England.

"But I was completely wrong. Biology is not my forte, so I leave that failure to anthropologists to explain. The obvious one, which I advance with diffidence, is that the human cerebrum has not yet acquired (in 112,846 B.C.) those racial convolutions indispensable for rational, concentrated thought. Natural selection, or its evolutional equivalent, apparently needs a few more thousands of years. At best, it was like trying to teach a chimpanzee how to use a camera. In spite of fingers more than facile enough to trip the shutter, vision and reflexes able to observe and identify a subject, it will never master the instrument. The relation of light to lens and film is too abstract for the animal; it will never take a good photograph except by chance.

"I failed ludicrously with the children. Years were wasted on devising various new educational methods before I could accept the result as foreordained. At most my pupils were a little more fluent than their uneducated fellows; writing of any sort they were unable to master, although, oddly enough, they produced quite appealing pictures. I still cannot see why the step from pictures to words proved impossible. As for mathematics—counting, merely—my prize student won that title by learning to achieve a correspondence between his fingers and a group of not more than three objects. Like monkeys, they couldn't or wouldn't pay attention, and no learning is possible without it.

"If I had been supplied with books, music, or suitable companionship, I might never have nerved myself to attempt the job alone. But there was nothing to do except observe, experiment, and record. In the course of twenty-eight years I have written thirty-two long reports, each of which, like this one, lists in the appendix the locations of all earlier data, in terms of astronomical constants.

"But to return to the crux of this particular investigation, the most important of all. Even though there was little prospect that humanity could profit at this time from a steam power plant, I determined not to abandon the project. I built a steam engine. It took me twelve years. Make no mistake: with all my technical training, and I have always been as much of an engineer as a physicist, it still took that long. Every single part had to be made by hand—my hand. But even before it could be made, raw materials had to be prospected, dug, transported, processed, and shaped.

"Occasionally I persuaded or bullied my proto-human subjects to act as beasts of burden, but most of the labor was necessarily my own. And let me assure you that the engine was flawlessly designed and constructed. Parts requiring close tolerance were hand-ground and polished, once for over two hundred hours. Details and sketches will be found in the appendix. Let them be checked by experts; I know there are no defects. After all, I've had years, literally, in which to make sure of my work. You may wonder why I stress this point; it is not mere vanity, God knows. The astounding conclusion of this report depends completely on the soundness of my power plants. If they are faulty, my inference, hard enough to accept in any case, is invalid.

"That high pressure engine was completed nearly a decade ago. It was perfect in every respect, yet when I opened the valve to admit high pressure steam, the results confounded all my eager anticipations. The tubular boiler is oil-fired; the piston is like glass in its almost frictionless motion; everything is as it should be. Yet the power is only forty per cent of the calculated amount. Every re-calibration of my test instruments—themselves the painstaking work of many months— failed to explain the discrepancy.

"Baffled by this anomalous performance, but with full confidence in my engineering skill, I resolved to construct a simple dynamo to be operated by the steam engine. It was my intention to use a battery of electrical test instruments in an independent determination of the engine's power.

"Building a dynamo was easier than the preceding job, because of my hard-earned knowledge of primitive expedients, but by no means a small undertaking. Five more years went by before I finished. Oddly enough, wire was by far the worst problem; only a man who has had to draw uniform copper wire single-handed can appreciate that fact.

"I felt very elated when the critical moment came, and the dynamo was coupled to my unaccountably lame steam engine. You can probably guess the outcome: *No current flowed*. Not a single ampere. I rechecked the windings a dozen times. I will hardly be accused of conceit for saying that to me the theory of an electric generator is like that of the simple lever to Lord Kelvin. In the appendix is a diagram of my machine. It will be found correct in design. Yet, I repeat, there was no current to be had. Further—and this was almost terrifying—the steam engine spun the generator's shaft without a trace of resistance. You know what that implies. When lines of magnetic force are cut, work is done, and there *must* be resistance.

"You can make the unique inference now. The steam engine works feebly. A generator fails altogether. I vouch for the engineering of both. Unless I have somehow lost my mind in this time shift, the machines should work, and at full efficiency compatible with their designs.

"Only one conclusion seems possible, however hard to accept emotionally. Nature is simply not *ready* in 112,874 B.C. for these devices. When man's mental development is such that his most superior individuals: Heron, Newcomen, Watt, Faraday, begin to tinker with steam and electricity, *then* full efficiency, even though not approximated for centuries, will be—how shall I put it?—waiting for their genius.

"Since there is no man—or shouldn't be—capable of conceiving and building a generator in the 1,129th Century B.C., neither is a full-blown magnetic field attainable which will yield current when its lines of force are cut. The residual magnetism needed to prime my dynamo maintains a feeble existence, but electric power itself lies in the future. Evidently Peirce was right, and physical laws evolve just as does life.

"This will probably be my last report. I am suffering from a number of degenerative diseases for which no drugs are available. Yesterday I had a mild heart attack. For a man of eighty-five, I have managed well enough these last months; but the end must be near. I am burying this report tonight. If no later message turns up, this is farewell."

In a profound hush, Raymond left the lectern. There was no whispering; no applause. Even Dr. Matison's cat-footed return to the stage was clearly audible in the back rows. He stood there for a moment, unwilling to shatter the potent silence. Finally, however, he spoke.

"We are searching for Sir Walter's other reports. I need not emphasize their unique value. Unfortunately, although the stars and planets move according to rigorously predictable forces, the Earth's surface does not; and the boxes have almost certainly shifted great distances in 115,000 years.

"I can inform the Society," he continued, "that Mannering's specifications have been carefully studied by a committee under Dr. Kaelin, and they report his engineering to be unexceptionable in every way. But for a few minor improvements in alloys and insulation, our best work is hardly superior to his.

"It isn't necessary to point out the importance of this report relative to our own critical problem of declining power. It seems obvious that if natural forces evolve from nothingness to maturity, they may also degenerate with the passage of centuries. The steam power that became adult with James Watt is now in its senescence; Faraday's lines of force are also dying. Atomic fuel, still vigorous, is scarce and expensive. Much of the world still depends on steam and electricity. Are we then to abandon hope? I cannot believe so. I cannot think of death without birth.

"Somewhere about us, hitherto undetected, indeed, undreamed of, some *new* species of natural power may be emerging from its infancy. It is our task to find that infant prodigy and put it to work. In that search, this Society will, I'm sure, play a major part.

"This meeting stands adjourned."

Security

"For ten minutes with these papers," said Dr. Mason, stroking the bright-eyed kitten on his lap, "the enemy would gladly pay a million dollars."

The naval officer frowned uneasily. "That much, really?" A wry smile touched his lips. "There can't be very many men in the world who could make anything of your notes in ten minutes—or ten hours, either, for that matter."

"I meant, of course, they'd give plenty to get an expert here in this room for a few days. And don't think for a second that they haven't dozens of scientists who'd catch on damn quick once they saw this math." He waved a sheaf of papers. "There's Vavilov, Hsui, and quite a few others. Never underestimate your opponent: isn't that a military axiom, Commander? We should know our enemy by now; too much misevaluation in the past surely taught us a lesson in that regard." He raised the loudly purring kitten to his desk, where it humped its back comically, sprang into the air, and plunked with all claws extended squarely on an imposing looking stack of documents. A corner fluttered, to be instantly pinned.

The officer watched disapprovingly. He was a dog man himself. Vague notions of fidelity, courage, and other military virtues passed through his mind.

Dr. Mason guessed his attitude, and chuckled, giving the commander an amused glance.

"You sailors," he complained, "naturally prefer the loyal dog to the eccentric, independent cat. It's easy to figure a dog; he wears his heart on his sleeve, and always obeys orders. Man is his god, an attitude some people enjoy. I won't offend you by explaining why! But just catch a cat doing what it's told. As for courage, I've seen many a small cat fight against terrible odds when its blood was up. It won't defend its master's boots, though.

"However, I didn't mean to rehash the old battle. Security's the thing, and I'm unhappy; that's the main reason I asked you to come. Without boasting, I know that if the Sino-Soviets had my calculations on the Gravitational Field Generator, they could attack within a year— and almost certainly win. Why, with it you can stop missiles cold over a city of any size; and as for powering spaceships, a new era is in sight. No more weighing each ounce that goes into a rocket; no weight limit—none."

The commander's eyes narrowed. "Don't worry about security," he said in a sharp voice. "Hell, man, not even an invisible midget could slip in here without being blasted." He began to tick off points on his fingers.

"One—force. There are two battalions of crack troops quartered right on the grounds, fully armed, and on twenty-four-hour alert. Any raiding party strong enough to crash through could never reach this area undetected; they'd be annihilated by the Seventh Corps, with fifty thousand top combat men to draw from.

"Two—detector-security. There isn't a chance for spy-rays or micro-pickups. Every inch of this plant was built expressly to make all such devices useless. And even if our own detectors missed something, we have a scrambling beam going constantly that will jam any broadcast up to a million watts. Can you imagine anybody smuggling a more powerful transmitter than that into here? One that size would weigh tons. No, just let 'em try sending anything out of here!

"Three—personnel. How can they plant a spy in this installation when psycho-technicians can shoot a man full of drugs and probe him from his bald spot clear down to his toes—and back to his memories of the womb. I've seen them do it. One man confessed to stealing a nickel's worth of candy when he was nine years old!"

"No doubt," Dr. Mason admitted, taking the kitten back in his lap. "But somehow I've been uneasy. I have a queer feeling of being watched. I'm getting jumpy."

"Of course, you're being watched. We keep an eye on everybody."

"I don't mean that; I should be used to your spies by now."

"You're just working too hard. You should relax more often."

Mason snorted. "They won't let me out except with a heavy guard of your bully-boys for fear somebody'll blast me. Never even have a visitor without days of clearance. I used to slip out for a walk in the park, or a night at the opera, but two years ago they clamped down. The damned generator, I suppose; they're terrified the enemy will get wind of it. Well, I'm tired of other scientists for company, and the only non-intellectual I can associate with is my kitten. Just look at Fermi." He pointed to his pet. "That's the temperament I need. No nerves there. Uninhibited, graceful. Never tense except for an immediate utilitarian act, then wholly relaxed the instant after."

The commander watched him stroke the soft fur, vague annoyance growing in his mind. These experts were a tiresome responsibility: high strung, unreasonable. Obviously there wasn't a spy within hundreds of miles. Too bad the military couldn't invent its own equipment. He glanced enviously at the door leading to Mason's luxurious suite. Nothing was too good for a top research man. Sudden, irrational malice moved him, although, paradoxically, he was fond of the scientist.

"One of these days," he warned sourly, "that cat will tear up your best work, or"—with a chuckle—"commit a nuisance right over those nightmare matrices there!"

Dr. Mason grinned, the tired lines about his eyes deepening to crow's feet. "Not on your life. Cats don't behave that way. This one was probably housebroken by its mother, as usual. Clean right from the start." He waggled a bit of string before the kitten, and although the paw-stroke seemed a mere lazy swipe, hooked claws captured the string before it could be whisked away. It settled on the desk.

"What if your men had muscles like Fermi here?" he demanded proudly, as if personally responsible for the animal's natural endowments. "What a navy you could develop if men had strength and agility in the same ratio to weight as this little rascal. Especially in space, where so much coddling will be needed."

"Don't forget," the commander objected, "ours is a pushbutton military, and no organism can match a well-designed robot for reactive speed and precision."

"That's true, on the whole, but quick, independent action by a free agent will always be needed in some emergency situations. And no robot can be built to handle all the variations arising in combat. I remember when a Loki ICBM with an H-bomb in its nose ran wild over Los Angeles. The 'destruct' button didn't work, nobody knows why, and a dozen of the big brass sat there frozen waiting for the county to blow off the map. It was no robot but a Lieutenant J. G. who thought of getting a new anti-missile missile after it in a hurry. A few more seconds of delay, and Los Angeles would be a memory. That officer looked like a commander I know, but he wasn't so fond of robots then!"

The commander flushed with pleasure. "That was some years ago, when missiles were full of bugs. Now we have foolproof relays and duplicate controls. A child could handle our biggest hardware safely. It couldn't happen today. No, muscle speed is obsolete; it can't possibly compete with electronic units."

"Never believe it. No robot has all the flexibility of a living, sentient organism. The Reds are better at missile design and theory than we—yes, it's true; we needn't bluff to each other, not in here— yet they train their young men more rigorously by far. Old-fashioned muscle exercise, too."

"Maybe so," the officer said stubbornly. "But a whole army of cat-men would be useless without a robot technology. A bullet or explosive wave is still faster than any animal; so is a radar pulse. All men are good for, really, is to *be* there, in certain key places, just in case. Perhaps the robots loaf when nobody's looking," he added facetiously. "In fact, it's only because of the machines you scientists can dream up that the government coddles you so. Anything you like from steak at five dollars a pound to Hollywood starlets for company," he concluded mendaciously. "Except, of course, freedom to live naturally."

"Yes, isn't it ironical that when people fight for survival, they must deprive themselves of almost all the things worth living for?"

"Count your blessings," the commander said darkly. "Maybe in ten more years—if the peace balance holds on the present knife-edge—even adopting a kitten will involve so much red tape you'll settle for some new three dimensional TV Feelie-Smellie Set. Still," he added hastily, "it's only a temporary restriction."

Dr. Mason raised his brows. "Twenty-two years. More than one-fourth the average life time. Cold war and restriction of freedom in varying degrees." He sat in silence. The kitten sprang from the desk into his lap, and curled up, nose in its paws. The furry sides heaved gently; the delicate white whiskers twitched. He stroked the small form absently, his thoughts far away.

The officer cleared his throat harshly, and Dr. Mason started.

"Sorry," he said. "I'm being rude." The kitten squeaked in protest as he placed it on the floor. "I'll redeem myself by giving you a preview of our prize package. Come along."

He led the commander down a concrete corridor, unlocked a heavy metal door, and ushered the officer into a large laboratory. He pointed to an impressively-shrouded machine that bulked in one corner.

"There she is," he said proudly.

Together they stripped off the plastic cover, discussing the monster in enthusiastic tones. Finally Dr. Mason shrugged, made several adjustments, and peered about.

"This is hardly correct procedure," he said. "I'm not supposed to demonstrate until the big brass arrives. Besides, all the test equipment's being re-calibrated in another lab, so I'll have to improvise. But I can trust you; at least, if I can't, the whole security program's a farce. And you are anxious to see the generator in action, I presume."

"Damn right," was the eager reply. "If this contraption performs according to Hoyle, let the Sino-Soviets strike—it'll be the last time!"

"I'd just as soon they didn't," Mason demurred bitterly. "And the last time for whom?" He seized a squat metal stool, and placed it on a concrete slab. "I'll flatten this out for you," he promised in casual tones. "How many g's should that take, do you suppose?"

The officer's eyes twinkled as he studied the massive piece of furniture. "Humph. That'll need a lot of mass. I know these official stools—and the big, bureaucratic bottoms they uphold so valiantly! If you do it under five hundred pounds, I'll eat the fragments."

Mason nodded. "You haven't lost your engineering eye; take at least that." He put a pound weight directly top center of the stool, and returned to the machine. There he sighted carefully, set a dial, and pressed a stud. The stool settled itself firmly, metal legs digging into the concrete like an animal crouching to spring. As the commander watched in breathless fascination, Mason began to turn the dial. Steel creaked; the legs bowed slightly, but the tough material refused to yield.

"Five hundred g's won't do it; that's obvious," Mason said. "Typical government specifications—twice as high as ordinary commercial stuff." With an impatient gesture, he gave the dial a sharp clockwise twist. "Now we'll see."

There was a groan of overstressed metal, a loud snap, and one leg buckled. The stool tilted too fast for the eye to follow, and the pound weight, now equal to a ton, grated free.

"Look out!" The commander leaped back. Metal struck concrete with a force of two thousand pounds. Both men ducked, making themselves small, and a jagged hunk of concrete, chipped from the heavy slab, catapulted by to fall behind the officer with a strangely muffled sound.

White-lipped, the scientist sprang forward.

"Oh, Lord!" he groaned. "The kitten!"

From under the large fragment of concrete a tail-tip protruded. It twitched feebly for a moment, then stopped.

"Poor little devil," Mason muttered, his voice filled with regret. "What a lousy break—a one in a million chance."

"At least it was quick," the commander comforted him. "Never felt a thing, I'd bet."

"It was my fault," Mason accused himself. "I didn't notice he was following me in here. I should have remembered; he always did. If I …" He gaped. "Look! It's still moving! He's alive under there! The kitten's alive!"

They stared incredulously. The massive chunk of concrete stirred. It rose one inch, then another; it was pushed steadily aside. There was no blood; no torn flesh. The kitten stood up. It lurched away. Abruptly its wavering course straightened. Mewing, the little animal crouched.

"It can't be," the officer breathed. "Alive after that—and walking!"

"Maybe that concrete had a hollow underneath—no, that's not possible; look at the slab. Pounds of concrete on its back, and no blood, no—" He broke off, wild-eyed. The kitten spoke. From deep in its interior came a tiny, resonant voice—the words of Mason himself. They listened in unbelief.

"Kramer!" it cried exultantly. "The theory was right after all. We just miscalculated the field correction factor. It should be pi to gamma of xi, rather than—" The kitten whirred softly, and after a moment meowed—a plaintive, musical note, infinitely appealing. Once more the animal crouched, silent and tense.

"Commander," Mason gritted, appalled. "It's a robot—a damned enemy robot—and it's got our secret data recorded inside!"

"We'll see about that!" the officer snapped, leaping towards the motionless kitten. Instantly the tiny robot awoke to savage life, bounding insanely about the lab. Snarling, it clawed first at the door, then at the plastic windows.

"Look out—it mustn't get away!" Mason roared. "Ah, I've got it." Then he yelped in pain, staring horrified at his torn, bloody hands. "I couldn't hold it," he moaned. "Don't touch it—the damned thing's using full power now! You'll be clawed to ribbons."

"You're right!" The officer snatched a heavy wrench from a table, and coolly measured his swing. There was a crash as steel shattered concrete, but the robot shot by unharmed. Human muscles were no match for its incredible speed. It returned to a window, clawing frantically at the glowing plastic. Great shreds tore free under savage talon strokes.

"The guard!" Mason cried, leaping towards the door.

"No! Don't open it. If we let it out, there'll be no stopping it."

"But there's no alarm in the lab itself. We never thought—"

"We were wrong," the commander rasped. "Can't those fool sentries tell something is the matter?"

"No, not with one-way windows and all this soundproofing. It's up to us. Keep it away from the windows with that wrench; he won't tangle with it." Mewing, the robot retreated from the heavy tool. "That's the idea. Now, give me your jacket—quick, man!"

The commander blinked. Then, with a grunt of approval, he slipped off the ribboned blouse. Mason snatched it, and as the kitten raced by, opened it wide to bar the path. In an effortless, soaring leap, the robot sailed over Mason's head, one taloned paw ripping his scalp. Growling and spitting, the kitten flashed from floor to bench to generator, where it crouched, eyes glaring, fur on end.

"It's just too damned fast," the officer groaned.

"Once more," Mason snapped. "Go after him with the wrench again. I doubt if he's vulnerable, really, but they made him not to take chances."

The commander warily approached the generator, bludgeon ready. For a moment the kitten held its ground, then with a spiteful snarl resumed its wild round.

Mason wiped blood from his eyes, only to smear more from his injured hands. He held the tunic deliberately low as a feint, sweeping it up even before the kitten leaped. The anticipation trick worked. "You've got him!" the commander yelled, as Mason staggered under the impact. "Hold on!"

Breathing heavily, Mason kneeled on the writhing bundle, adding fold after fold. They heard muffled mewing; cloth ripped.

"My dress blouse," the officer complained ludicrously. "Give me a clear swing. Ah!" He brought the wrench down once, twice—smashing blows delivered with all his power. The cloth still heaved. "Like hitting steel springs," he panted. "It's tearing out."

"Hold on just for a second," Mason urged, leaping to the generator. Sighting hastily, he turned the dial, and the officer felt his own weight become unbearable. At Mason's gesture, he released his grip on the blouse, and gasping with the effort, crawled free of the squirming bundle. Immediately Mason gave the dial another twist. The movements were very small with the increased mass.

"It weighs half a ton now," Mason said grimly. "That'll keep the thing quiet." He paused. "Better not take any chances." Once more he turned the dial, and there were splintering sounds under the cloth. "Damnation!" he muttered. "Watch the thing while I lower the power."

Gradually he cut down the number of g's, and it was soon apparent that the robot was smashed. When they removed the ripped tunic, the kitten lay there quietly, its mechanisms shattered. They stared in wonder at the tiny cameras that had lain behind the kitten's guileless green eyes, together with the solar batteries which had supplied its energy. There were minute recorders with their hair-thin silvery wires on microscopic reels; and dozens of Duval motors that had driven those superb muscle-springs.

Mason looked up to meet the commander's dazed glance.

"Talk about robots," the officer said. "This is a Sino-Soviet job, and a humdinger. We've done a little along this line, but—" He shook an admiring head. "What do you think of robots now?"

"It's a beauty, all right, but they missed one thing. If it had played dead, after the concrete fell, we'd have buried it, I suppose. Then it could have dug its way out, and easily escaped at night—with all our data. But their robot didn't know enough—couldn't possibly. A living thing dies because it must; but how can a robot know that a kitten simply cannot survive with ten pounds of concrete on its back?"

A Touch of Sun

(Written with Irwin Porges)

When they wrecked his wooden shack to begin work on the steel tower, Professor Tincan's attitude suddenly changed. Until the actual razing, the old man had continued to wage a hopeless battle, a very vigorous one, although entirely verbal, as befits a slight man of sixty. But now, as they flung the sun-dried boards that had been his home to the foot of East Knoll, the professor became quiet and shrunken, a picture of bereavement.

The burly, competent steelworkers, stoical in the pounding desert heat, began their work ruthlessly; to them, Time was the only opponent. But they were not unsympathetic to the professor's sorrow. After all, the old man had lived in the wooden hut on top of the knoll for almost forty years. Not that he had any legal right to the ground; the owners of the vast Santa Teresa Ranch had merely ignored his existence from the beginning. If they thought of him at all, it was as a fixture of the property—like the stand of eucalyptus trees—and quite harmless to their interests, since this part of the ranch produced only ceramic clays and a few minerals.

Nevertheless, while they tolerated the solitary eccentric on their property, they had not the slightest intention of permitting sentiment to interfere with progress. So when Continental Electronics decided that East Knoll was an ideal location for one of the new remote-control television relay towers, the Santa Teresa management cheerfully accepted a generous fee, and gave the word that displaced Professor Tincan forever.

One official of Continental, it is true, did remark casually to a Fourth Vice President that some old nut had actually been living on

East Knoll alone for humpty-nine years, and that perhaps the company ought to make a gesture—you know, public relations, Walt—

"Nonsense!" was the Great Man's reply. "He hasn't a legal leg to stand on. Give that type any encouragement, and you're up against a nuisance suit. Just run him out of there, B.J.; that's my advice."

Since the fight seemed definitely lost, the professor grimly dragged the remains of his shack into a neat pile at the foot of the knoll. The heap of wood was dwarfed by one of metal, for there too was the huge collection of flattened tin cans that had earned the professor his name. From the time he had settled down on the little hill, he had saved every tin can that came his way, removing the label and ends, stamping the resulting tube flat, and even scouring the metal bright with dry sand. The truckers, a genial, open-handed lot, passing the ranch on the government highway, half a mile west, always dropped off canned goods for the professor, gratis. If the old man had tasted any fresh food in the last forty years, there was no record of the event. Beans, corn, tuna, fruit—it was all welcome. And the great accumulation of tin-coated steel, alternate stacks of round end-pieces and mashed cylinders, covered fifty or more feet in orderly piles.

But now, sitting there day after day, too depressed apparently to rebuild the lumber into another shelter, the old man watched bleakly as the tower thrust its way two hundred feet into the cloudless sky.

There was something about his silent, inscrutable gaze that annoyed the Chief Engineer. Unlike the crew, he could not take heat philosophically; he was also a bully, using either fists or tongue as the occasion seemed to require.

For the moment, however, there was a truce between the tower—a metal giant standing arrogantly on four massive girders set deep into concrete—and the small sexagenarian with his fluffy white hair and mild blue eyes. It is even possible that hostilities might never have resulted if another engineer had been in charge, for in his normal state of mind, the professor would never have dreamed of battling the great tower. Beside it he felt puny and helpless, and even had moments of perverse admiration for its utilitarian sturdiness.

But the job was Joel Hoffman's; he didn't like bums who took no part in the work of the world. There was so much to be done in the way of building, and he longed to have a share in all of it. Perhaps, too, he remembered his own father, shiftless and erratic, and the boy who was earning his way, unassisted, at sixteen. No, Hoffman had little patience with those who sat out the game.

"Hey, Professor," the engineer baited him each morning. "They're still waitin' on you at Harvard. Can I tell 'em it's okay?"

The old man would stare at him with cold-eyed detestation, his lips locked, but Hoffman knew all too well how to breach that wall of self-control, really a frail barrier.

"Got the letter right here, haven't I, boys?" he would add, waving an envelope, his face a picture of unselfish pleasure. "They've even raised the ante—you can get twelve thousand a year. They're not so dumb; they know you're the top man in this country for the job—Head of the big new Department of Tincanology! Yeah, Tincanology, how about that, gang? And they want that priceless collection of yours, too." Here he waved at the hundreds of metal sheets shimmering in the sun. "You know—for their museum."

At this the victim couldn't help wincing. He realized that saving tin cans for forty years is at best a highly eccentric habit, but what could he do about it? Like people who feel they must step on every crack in the sidewalk, he simply had no choice. It was literally impossible for him to throw a single can away, although he knew there was no possible use he could ever make of them.

"Ah, I understand," Hoffman persisted, looking concerned. "He ain't got enough dough to get there." He turned to the crew. "Or clothes, either. Say, is that a flour sack he's wearing? If so it's out of style, Grampa—discontinued brand. If only he was not so proud—he hates to cadge, right, boys? Lemme see. I got the solution for you. They tell me tin's in short supply again, so why not sell all this and go to Harvard in style? Hey, Johnson, bring the torch over, and let's melt this down for Grampa."

Grinning, the steel-worker would tug at the wheeled welding equipment, and horrified, the professor would run to defend his precious cans.

"Never mind, Johnson. Harvard ain't offerin' enough. He's waitin' on Cal Tech." It was all very labored, and some of the men didn't find it funny, but J.H. was the boss, so what the hell.

What made it particularly hilarious was the old man's incoherence, for after half a century the nerve paths joining brain and vocal chords had almost atrophied through disuse. His voice, high-pitched and jerky, was like a rusty, neglected machine that ran feebly for a time, then grated to a halt. But a more perceptive man than the engineer might have found something to ponder in the professor's choice of words, which were out of keeping with the illiterate old derelict they thought him.

Once the old man became so angry that he hurled half a dozen of his cherished cans at Hoffman, scaling them in flat, dangerous trajectories with an accuracy that suggested a very good eye. But the engineer, light on his feet for a heavyweight, had merely dodged, laughing, and then with calm malice, despite the professor's stricken look, sailed them down into a brushy draw. It had taken the victim two hours to recover five; the sixth remained lost, although he searched until dark.

And always the tower grew, like some fabulous tropical tree, several feet daily; it squatted insolently where the weathered shack had been. Before long they were welding on the three horizontal cross-members which made the steel pyramid resemble a six-armed Martian giant. Soon the tower proper would be complete, and work could begin on the complex and immensely valuable electronic units it was built to house.

They finished the steel skeleton on schedule; Hoffman saw to that, driving the crew hard, ubiquitous himself. He gave them no time to reconstruct the professor's shack, as a few of the men had planned to do. They gathered their equipment in the heavy truck, and crawled down the unimproved road towards the highway. A lighter vehicle, with better springs, brought up the electronic assemblies.

Watching sullenly, the professor saw a fortune in copper, silver, and germanium packed into the giant's cranium: tubes, transistors, huge crystals, all meticulously patterned two hundred feet above the sand. Then this phase, too, was done. After the week-end holiday, the

132

lower components would be instaled, and the relay tower ready for performance tests. Even then, if the engineer had not persisted …

"Hey, Professor," he barked, one dusty foot on the truck's hub-cap. The hunched figure by the stacks of tin cans gave him a brief, cryptic glance. "I'm not sure our li'l ol' tower's safe alone with you until Monday. For two cents I'd run you out of here. He doesn't like us, not one damn bit. A sour old bird. A touch of the sun, that's his trouble. Suppose he gets really mad, and kicks over the whole job. Think of all our hard work wasted!" He pretended to plead. "I'm sorry, Grampa, if I've hurt your feelin's. Please don't wreck the tower the minute we leave. Costs over $200,000. Be a sport, Prof—promise me you won't hurt it."

"Why not, Hoffman?" one of the men demanded. "More time-and-half."

"Yeah, maybe for you, knucklehead—I'd get canned."

"You mean tin-canned, J.H."

Here the old man's head rose a little in a sharp, birdlike motion, and the engineer felt a sudden stir of alarm. Maybe it wasn't so funny; what if the guy—? His mind quickly reviewed technical details of the construction: the huge girders, four of them, set a full five yards into tough concrete—this was earthquake country. And the careful welds; Johnson was tops at those; they would be stronger than the original metal. No, it was absurd. Even if one of the supports failed—but who could injure a single girder, much less destroy it? The little old bum had nothing but a few hand tools to work with; certainly there was no heavy stuff within twenty miles—no torches, no explosives. As for the delicate parts that were all too vulnerable, they were two hundred feet up. Few able-bodied men could climb half that high. For a man of sixty or so—he must be crack-brained to entertain such a weird idea about the professor even momentarily. Imagine the guy wrecking a twenty-story, all steel, welded tower with just a hammer and a screwdriver!

The engineer gave the recluse a derisive, valedictory wave, shouted "Stay in the shade, Grampa—your trouble's too much sun!" and climbed into the cab. In three minutes the old man was alone—he and his mighty, dumb protagonist, the six-armed, four-legged monster of steel.

Chief Engineer Hoffman was restless Sunday. He couldn't get Professor Tincan off his mind. Over and over he reviewed the situation. His mind said "impossible," but still a tiny alarm bell in his brain rang a peremptory, nagging warning. Finally, although he wasn't due back on the job until Monday morning at eight, Hoffman gave into the irrational impulse that wouldn't be quelled, and by noon Sunday was in his station wagon heading for the Santa Teresa Ranch.

He should have been able to see the top of the tower from the highway; thought he knew just where to look—he gulped at the sight of blank, glaring sky. Swearing, he jammed the accelerator to the floor, tooling the car up the rough road with a jolting, creaking disregard for his safety. What he saw at East Knoll made his stomach contract like a fist. The tower was down! Like the bones of some stricken titan the steel members strewed the arid ground.

Slamming on the brakes, he leaped out of the car and ran to the top of the knoll. He stood there aghast, uncomprehending. Obviously, two of the great girders had been cut, and the others, unable to take the enormous, unbalanced stress, had failed. But cut how? It looked like a torch job, but that simply wasn't conceivable. How could the professor, without so much as a wheelbarrow, bring heavy equipment twenty miles or more? And who would lend valuable tools to a man in rags without a dime? Professor Tincan! Hoffman realized for the first time that the old man had vanished. Surely that meant guilt. Fuming, the engineer began to prowl the deserted camp, searching for some clue to the tower's destruction. Nothing but a hammer, boards—and the damned tin cans all over the place. Furiously he scattered the stacks with his feet. He must know how the professor had done it. He'd have him put away for good.

Once more Hoffman ranged over the area, unable to spot a single lead. Why, it was even obvious from the tire marks that no other vehicles had been near the site since the crew left on Friday. That meant no heavy stuff could have been used at all. And yet the tower was down—surely no hammer was responsible for that grim fact. Nor were the few data any clearer—boards, tin cans, some nails—and the shattered steel enclosing a frightful mess which hours earlier had been the finest electronic units in the state.

He was still trying, baffled but persistent, when night came.

On Friday evening, just after Hoffman and the crew had left for the week-end, the professor might have been found studying the tower with concentrated hate in his eyes, now a harder, more opaque blue. Right where one of its four girders was rooted had been his favorite spot, just outside the hut. He had always enjoyed sitting there with his back against the warm wood, watching the stars make their timeless circles across the sky. And now, as if in brutish contempt, this immovable titan stood with one great foot spurning that very bit of ground.

Consumed with sudden, blind fury, the professor snatched his hammer and struck repeated full-armed blows against the unyielding metal. The cracked, dull notes had neither melody nor sonority; rather they seemed to him like the witless, jeering laughter of an idiotic giant, utterly scornful of his impotence. Raging, the old man flung the tool aside. Here he was, alone with his enemy for more than forty-eight hours, and yet powerless to bring it down.

After a moment's brooding thought, he rummaged in a wooden box, and produced a hacksaw. He made a few tentative cuts—scratches, really—on a girder, then the blade snapped. Small wonder; it was twenty-seven years old. But the professor knew very well that even with an unlimited supply of new ones, all his remaining years of life would not be enough to topple so massive a structure that way. No, there was nothing he could do.

Following a typical meal—a pound of kidney beans, cold from a can, which he flattened and added almost mechanically to the smallest stack—the old man seated himself by the pile of boards and watched the red sun drop with ever increasing velocity behind the foothills. Distorted, but still hot, it rested for an instant on top of a cluster of live oaks, changing them to fiery skeleton trees. Then it plunged behind the crest, and the desert night had come. But not before the professor had his inspiration.

When he stood up, his petulance had vanished, and the single stare he gave his steel adversary, towering so calmly invulnerable above him, was almost compassionate. Enemy it might be, this six-armed invader that had planted its metal feet on his home, but merely, after all, a creature of Continental Electronics, an organization he personified in Hoffman. A $200,000 lackey, the tower, soon to crash in ruins at the hands of an old man. Such was Professor Tincan's dream. An indemnity for his house and his pride. A blow at the Chief Engineer. Not full measure, but something.

It was hard to sit quietly, waiting for the bright desert moon, but he couldn't work in the dark, and had never used artificial illumination in the hut, going to bed with the sun on those nights when staying outside was unattractive. Thinking about details of his plan, however, helped the time to pass quickly, and after a while a silver light, strong enough for his purpose, threw the tower's shadow across the sand.

Hurriedly, but with a precision that would have intrigued the engineer, Professor Tincan began to build. Under his amazingly deft fingers, which seemed to have recaptured a facility untapped for decades, the old man put together, from the boards of his shack, thin and well-seasoned, a light, strong framework. It was shaped roughly like a bowl eight feet across, but scientifically skeletonized, so that its weight was moderate. With more wood and hinges from the doors and shutters, he mounted this hollow hemisphere on a stand so sturdy and ingenious that by swiveling a long counterweighted plank he could move the bowl to almost any position and keep it there with little effort.

There was a slight smile on his face now. This was like being back in the lab—1920, that would be—under the great Dr. Abbott. After that … but this was not the time for regrets.

With nails from the wooden chest the professor began to fasten bright, circular sheets of tin-plate to the frame, mounting each on a crude but workable pivot. Every now and then he paused to gaze at the tower, bulking black and impressive against the moon. He became aware, for the first time, of the forces at play in that sky-flung, almost sentient structure. Triangles were the basis of its strength: tension versus compression, alternating; and scrutinizing the geometric lacework of steel, he saw formulas writing themselves endlessly on the fabric of his brain. Against triangles he meant to pit parabolas, and surely the figure superior in the hierarchy of mathematics must prevail.

It was almost eleven in the morning when the basic work was done, and there was still the most exacting part to come. Under the rays of the sun, the old man began to adjust the dozens of shiny tin reflectors on their nail pivots, at the same time bending each sheet to proper curvature. There was a remarkable agreement between the geometry of his mind and its physical realization in the device before him. As he meticulously joined the forces of the individual units, the bright spot of reflected sunlight which each contributed merged with the others to form a glowing patch on the sand—a roughly square inferno about three inches on a side: the exact focus of the whole compound parabolic reflector. Before half the metal discs were adjusted, there was a pool of glassy slag smoking and bubbling in the center of the focal spot.

The sun grew hotter, the mighty desert sun, unimpeded by clouds or dust, which squanders millions of kilowatts of energy on the tortured soil, and still the little man, leathery skinned as a lizard, toiled on, unmindful of the glare.

At one-thirty, the hottest part of the day, when the last unit was aligned, the professor watched the boiling silicates at the end of the beam, and grinning, pranced like an excited gnome. Then he gripped the controlling plank, and in letters of molten sand wrote on the earth: "Fiat justicia; ruat coelum." For the prodigy of forty years ago had read Latin—and other languages—as most people read their newspapers.

"Let justice be done, though the heavens fall," he translated aloud for the benefit of the waiting giant. "But it's not the heavens that are going to fall," he added meaningly.

Moving with short, careful steps, he wrestled his solar furnace up the gentle slope of East Knoll towards the tower. Did the monster tremble at his approach? The professor felt sure that it did.

The man took a deep breath, gripped the counterbalance in grimy, blistered hands, and up from the vaporized sand, in a smooth, deadly arc, the fiery spot, well over 2,500 degrees centigrade, rose to deal with one of the four girders sustaining the steel structure.

"A touch of the sun," the professor said, remembering, a mirthless grin on his face, determination in his eyes.

Where that dazzling patch caressed metal there was a hissing coruscation; no welding torch could have burned any faster. Moving deliberately, more to prolong his triumph than because additional time was needed, he swung the reflector ten degrees from left to right. White sparks showered down, and the great pyramid sagged. Overhead there was the tortured shriek of rending metal, and one of the cross-members, tearing loose weld and all, fell with an earth-jarring crash twenty feet away.

The professor knew that he had won. A quarter of a million dollars in steel, electronic equipment, and man-hours of engineering lay crumpled on the hot sand.

Stepping up to the nearest fragment, and looking almost regretful, the professor put one tattered shoe on the chunk of steel in a vague gesture of victory.

Five minutes later the old man began breaking up his solar furnace. Never should the engineer have the satisfaction of knowing how a small, frail man of sixty, with no tools but a hammer and his brain, had leveled the magnificently constructed tower of steel.

When the tin sheets had been cunningly mixed with the others, in case the nail holes might betray his secret, the professor spread fresh sand over the Latin inscription and the pools of slag, gathered a few belongings, and headed for the Santa Ana hills. He was hardly aware that in laying low the tower he had abruptly lost his compulsion to save tin cans, and was abandoning the collection of a lifetime without a single qualm. Let Chief Engineer Hoffman make of the deserted stacks what he could. Before he read this riddle, the old man thought cheerfully, as he made for the highway, Hoffman would spend twice forty years here himself.

And the answer so simple. Just a touch of the sun!

Checklist of Sources

The checklist below gives the original publication source for each of the stories included in this collection:

"The Ruum," first published in *The Magazine of Fantasy and Science Fiction*, October 1953.

"The Rats," first published in *Man's World*, February 1951.

"The Fly," first published in *The Magazine of Fantasy and Science Fiction*, September 1952.

"By a Fluke," first published in *The Magazine of Fantasy and Science Fiction*, October 1955.

"Emergency Operation," first published in *The Magazine of Fantasy and Science Fiction*, May 1956.

"Story Conference," first published in *The Magazine of Fantasy and Science Fiction*, May 1953.

"The Logic of Rufus Weir," first published in *The Magazine of Fantasy and Science Fiction*, November 1955.

"The Entity," first published in *Fantastic Universe*, December 1955.

"Whirlpool," first published in *Fantastic Universe*, March 1957.

"The Unwilling Professor," first published in *Dynamic Science Fiction*, January 1954.

"Guilty as Charged," first published in *The New York Post*, November 27, 1955.

"The Mannering Report," previously unpublished.

"Security," first published in *Amazing Stories*, September 1959.

"A Touch of Sun," first published in *Fantastic*, April 1959.

About the Author

Arthur Porges was born in Chicago, Illinois on August 20, 1915. One of four brothers, he was educated at Roosevelt High School and Senn High School before enrolling at The Lewis Institute where he achieved a Bachelor of Science Degree in Mathematics. After the successful completion of his postgraduate studies, through which he attained Masters Degrees in Mathematics and Engineering from the Illinois Institute of Technology, Porges enlisted in the U.S. Army in 1942. During the Second World War he served as an artillery instructor, teaching algebra and trigonometry to field personnel. He was stationed at various military installations including Camp White in Oregon, Fort Sill, Oklahoma, Camp Roberts, California and at Barnes Hospital in Vancouver, Washington. After the war Porges returned to Illinois and taught mathematics at the Western Military Academy, going on to serve as an assistant professor at De Paul University. Having taught at Occidental College in Los Angeles for a brief stint in the late forties, Porges made a permanent move to California in 1951 and spent several years as a mathematics teacher at Los Angeles City College. During this period he wrote and sold short stories as a sideline. In 1957, Porges retired from teaching to write full-time. He went on to publish hundreds of short stories in numerous magazines and newspapers. Many of his stories appeared in *Alfred Hitchcock's Mystery Magazine*, *Ellery Queen's Mystery Magazine*, *Amazing Stories* and *The Magazine of Fantasy and Science Fiction*. His fiction spanned several genres, with tales ranging from science fiction and fantasy to horror, mysteries, and so on. At his most prolific his work was appearing in three or four periodicals in one month alone. Among his best-known stories are "The Ruum," "The Rats," "No Killer Has Wings," "The Mirror" and "The Rescuer." Eight previous book collections of his short stories have been published: *Three Porges Parodies and a Pastiche* (1988), *The Mirror and Other Strange*

Reflections (2002), *Eight Problems in Space: The Ensign De Ruyter Stories* (2008), *The Adventures of Stately Homes and Sherman Horn* (2008), *The Calabash of Coral Island and Other Early Stories* (2008), *The Miracle of the Bread and Other Stories* (2008), *The Devil and Simon Flagg and Other Fantastic Tales* (2009) and *The Curious Cases of Cyriack Skinner Grey* (2009). A keen birdwatcher and an avid reader, in later years Porges wrote many articles, essays and poems, most of which were published in the *Monterey Herald*. Several of his poems were collected in the book *Spring, 1836: Selected Poems* (2008). After spells in Laguna Beach and San Clemente, Porges moved north, eventually settling in Pacific Grove. He passed away, at the age of 90, in May 2006.

Printed in Great Britain
by Amazon

26435446R00085